"I'm not leaving you to travel through Mexico by yourself."

The very idea made Owen's blood pressure rise.

Bernadette patted his hand. "You're such a gentleman, but I've been taking care of myself for a long time. I've traveled to other foreign countries alone, my Spanish is fluent and I'm familiar with the culture. I'll really be safer without—"

"No, you would not be safer without me!" Owen protested. "Let's have this out once and for all. You claim to be so good at interpreting men. Did you not see the way that *federale* was looking at you?" He leaned in, nose to nose. "You. Are. Stuck. With. Me. Period."

* * *

THE TEXAS GATEKEEPERS:
Protecting the borders...and the women they love

Books by Elizabeth White

Love Inspired Suspense

Under Cover of Darkness #2
Sounds of Silence #11
On Wings of Deliverance #20

*The Texas Gatekeepers

ELIZABETH WHITE

A native Mississippian, Elizabeth White now lives on the Alabama Gulf Coast with her minister husband, two teenagers and a Boston terrier named Angel. Beth plays flute and pennywhistle in church orchestra, teaches second-grade Sunday school, and—as an occasional diversion from writing—paints portraits in chalk pastel. Creating stories of faith, in which a man and woman fall in love with each other and Jesus, is her passion and source of personal spiritual growth. She is always thrilled to hear from readers c/o Steeple Hill Books, 233 Broadway, Suite 1001, New York, NY, 10279 or on the Web at www.elizabethwhite.net.

ELIZABETH WHITE

On Wings *of* Deliverance

Steeple
Hill●

Published by Steeple Hill Books™

STEEPLE HILL BOOKS

Steeple
Hill®

ISBN 0-373-87360-3

ON WINGS OF DELIVERANCE

Copyright © 2006 by Elizabeth White

www.SteepleHill.com

Printed in U.S.A.

I sought the Lord, and He answered me;
He delivered me from all my fears. Those
who look to Him are radiant; their faces
are never covered with shame.
—*Psalms* 34:4–5

To Mary Ann,
who has prayed faithfully for this story.

ACKNOWLEDGMENTS

I would like to express my gratitude
to fellow author Jane Meyers Perrine,
who translated my Spanish when she had her own
stories to write. *¡Gracias!*

Appreciation also goes to
Karen M. Wise, whose entertaining and
often funny Internet journal of her bus adventure
through central Mexico enriched my story with
details. Great pictures!

Thanks to my children who put up with me during
marathon writing sessions. And to my husband, who
came through with great ideas and encouragement
when I needed it—all I can say is I love you!

ONE

Yucatán Peninsula, Mexico

"So there I am, all fat, dumb and happy—" Owen Carmichael ducked under the Cessna to check the propeller mechanism "—when my bird's engine goes out and I see the ground coming at me like a pie in the face."

Kyle Garrett, the fifteen-year-old missionary kid helping Owen with preflight inspection, gently set down the sand crab he'd been playing with. "So what'd you do?" His freckled face was alive with curiosity.

"About fifty feet off the ground, I pull the nose up real quick, like you rein in a horse. Hand me that wrench, would you?" Owen gestured toward the tool chest sitting on the sand near the boy's feet. "Then I adjust in the opposite direction so the tail won't slam into the ground. The wind creates enough lift on the blades to slow the landing."

"Man, that's so cool that you can fly a chopper *and* a plane." Kyle squatted under the wing to watch Owen work. "I'm gonna take flying lessons when I go back to the States for college."

"Tell you what, next trip down here I'll take you up for a lesson." Deep under the belly of the plane, Owen squinted into the bright sunlight that flooded the beach, which also functioned as a makeshift airstrip.

From Owen's perspective, the kid didn't have much to complain about. The Gulf of Mexico lay just twenty yards away, and the ocean spray left a pleasant salty taste on his lips. He wished he had a few more days to spend here before heading back to the south Texas desert.

Unfortunately, his vacation time was up. As a United States Border Patrol agent/BORSTAR specialist, he'd been uniquely qualified to make this supply run down to the coast of the peninsula for Mission Aviation Fellowship. He was glad to do it, not least because of the excuse to check up on Bernadette Malone. Benny had been here for a month as a hurricane-relief volunteer, and he'd missed her—more than he would admit to anyone but himself.

"Hey, Owen?" Kyle's voice cracked on the upswing. "Hasn't Benny been driving my dad's old Jeep?"

Owen turned his head, leaning down to keep from putting a dent in his forehead. All he could see were Kyle's bare knobby knees and the waves breaking on the beach. "Yeah, why?"

"I think that's her, coming in from the village."

Owen yanked a bolt. "Guess she wanted to say goodbye one more time." Ha, wishful thinking. Benny's goodbye to him this morning in the cafeteria had been sleepy—cranky to the point of hostility. She was not a morning person.

"She must be in an awful hurry. I've never seen her

do more than thirty, and she's spitting sand, driving like a maniac." Kyle crab-walked out from under the wing.

Owen pushed clear of the plane and stood up, sliding his shades onto his face. "Wow. Look at her go." The Jeep dodged in a zigzag pattern worthy of a stunt driver in an action film. Bernadette was the most cautious woman he knew. What would make her drive like this?

The Jeep skidded to a halt on the inland side of the beach, parallel to the plane's takeoff path. Benny hopped out and tore across the sand, arms and legs pumping and her long, curly hair flying like a black flag.

"Owen! I'm so glad you're still here!" She ran past him and yanked open the plane's passenger door.

"What are you doing?" Owen exchanged glances with a wide-eyed Kyle, then snagged Benny around the waist before she could clamber into the plane.

She shoved at his hands and seemed to notice Kyle for the first time. Her eyes widened. "Kyle, get out of here! Take the Jeep—head for the jungle!"

Kyle just gaped at her.

Owen grabbed her shoulders. "What's the matter with you?"

Her breath hissed through her teeth. "I'll explain when we're in the air. Owen, get me out of here! I don't want Kyle seen with me. Please, make him go!"

Owen couldn't see Benny's eyes behind her mirrored sunglasses. Her dark-olive skin was pasty.

"Owen!" Struggling to pull away, she burst into tears.

"Okay, okay." Bewildered, he let her go. "Kyle, take the Jeep off the road and head home the back way. I'll find out what's the matter and bring her later."

Kyle saluted and loped off toward his father's old vehicle.

Benny took a couple of hiccuping breaths. "There's a man trying to kill me. He said he was FBI—"

"What?" Was she kidding? Benny had a great sense of humor, but she rarely pulled practical jokes.

"She said they're coming after us both. You've got to take me with you!"

"Benny—" He shook his head. "I've got flight regulations. And you're supposed to stay for another two months, right?"

"Yes, but they'll just have to understand. Please, Owen, he's right behind—" She gasped and looked over Owen's shoulder, her face gray. "Here he comes! Come on, we've got to go!"

Owen turned. A dark-green Land Rover approached from the direction Benny had come. Something that looked a lot like a gun glinted in the sunlight just over the vehicle's windshield.

Good night.

"Benny, we've gotta get out of here."

"Ya think?" She turned, gathering the folds of her full floral skirt in one hand. Impractical in many ways but she was always careful to comply with the missionary dress code—modest tops, skirts past the knees and nothing tight. No pants.

Owen gave her a hand up into the plane, stowed the steps, then ran around to the pilot seat. He had just started the engine when something pinged off the wing with a screech of metal on metal.

Bullets.

He was used to smugglers along the border getting

excited about their little enterprises being busted up. But down here in paradise, you weren't supposed to get hurt—except maybe by renegade jellyfish.

Another round hammered the plane as it taxied. Increasing speed, Owen checked to make sure Benny was buckled in. At least she had that much sense. He put on his headphones and gestured for her to do the same.

Adjusting the elevators, he taxied faster and faster. The airstream caught the wings and the plane took to the sky, leaving the Land Rover on the beach.

Owen turned to Benny. She sat with her head back against the seat, fairly green around the mouth. "Now. You wanna tell me what that was all about?"

"Mom! Dad! You won't believe what just happened!"

Stacy Garrett, missionary nurse and wife of Dr. Wes Garrett, glanced over her shoulder when she heard the voice of her son, Kyle, shouting from outside the one-room clinic. She calmly held the thermometer in little Julio Carillo's mouth. Kyle got exited about the silliest things.

"In here, son," Wes called, meeting Stacy's gaze with twinkling eyes. "What's the matter?"

Kyle tore into the room, swinging on the doorjamb. "Benny just took off in Owen's plane!"

"Sweetie, we don't have time for your goofy jokes." Stacy patted the toddler's cheek. "Come get this bag of trash and take it out to the burn pile."

"Okay, but, Mom, I'm not kidding around. Did you know she was leaving today?" He walked over and grabbed the plastic bag under the window.

"Benny's got another two months before she goes back. Owen probably just took her up for a ride."

Kyle shook his head. "He was planning to leave as soon as he filed his flight plan. He was tinkering with something under the plane when she came tearing across the beach. She made me take the Jeep and come home the back way. She looked really scared, and she said—" he took a breath "—she didn't want me to be seen with her."

"I'm sure you misunderstood her." Wes paused over his patient, a woman with a tumor on her neck. "She'll be back later and explain what that was all about. Now do what your mother says and take out the trash."

Kyle reluctantly dragged the sack toward the door. "Okay, but I'm telling you something weird's going on. I heard some popping noises from the beach, like gunshots."

Wes dropped his stethoscope and gave Kyle a stern look. "Now you're being melodramatic. That Jeep's been backfiring for months. I don't want another word about it."

"All right." Kyle shrugged and hauled the trash over his shoulder. "But don't say I didn't tell you."

"What do you think's going on?" Stacy asked Wes as soon as Kyle was out of earshot. "There was that man who came to talk to Benny yesterday afternoon. She never said who he was or what he wanted."

"Benny's a very private young woman, Stace, but she's an incredible worker. It's not our place to interrogate her."

"It is if there's something wrong and we can help her. That's what the body of Christ is for. That man had a scary look in his eyes."

"And I think it's your overactive imagination. Give it a rest. Haven't you noticed the way Owen looks at Benny? What we've got here is some kind of courting ritual. I'm surprised you didn't see it."

Stacy rolled her eyes at her husband's smug look. "I didn't realize you were such a romantic. I'll leave it alone, but if she's not back here in a couple of hours, I'm calling her to make sure she's all right."

Benny had never been bothered by heights. Still, taking off while under fire was unnerving. And then there was the pilot....

Though reassured by his firm grasp of the control column, she found herself shaken by the way he looked at her. Those eyes, an unearthly gold-shot turquoise, always stuttered her brain.

Owen was a crack Border Patrol helicopter pilot. And she'd always been able to depend on him to help out at the orphanage back in Acuña. But how to explain what had sent her on this precipitate and dangerous exit from the village of Agrexco?

"Bernadette—" Owen's eyes narrowed as he turned his attention back to the control panel "—the FBI does not kill missionaries. And who's the 'she' that said they were after you?"

She cleared her throat. "I'm not sure who that guy was, but he wasn't FBI. I got an e-mail last night from an old friend saying that three of my oldest friends have died. I have to go back for—for the funerals."

"That's not the whole story, is it?"

Benny flinched at the hurt in his eyes. "Owen, I can't tell you everything. It's just too dangerous."

"More dangerous than some guy firing a submachine gun at us?"

He had a right to be indignant, but she couldn't formulate an answer that made sense. So she clamped her lips together and looked out the window. The bay underneath was blue and serene, and puffy clouds drifted past like a dream. How ironic.

Naturally, Owen wouldn't leave it alone. "What about the three friends dying all at once? How did that happen? Some kind of accident?"

"The e-mail wasn't very specific."

His mouth tightened. "Well, that's just great, Benny. People spill their guts to you all day long, but you never walk back across the bridge."

"What are you talking about?"

"I know exactly why you left Acuña to come all the way down to the Yucatán. You were afraid I was getting too close to you. Which is also why you've ignored me this whole week."

"I didn't ignore you! I was busy!" Benny clenched her hands. "We've had doctors and nurses and dentists needing translators and—"

"And I wanted to help, but you wouldn't let me. 'Go play with the children, Owen. Take this load of supplies over to the camp, Owen. I don't have time to talk right now....'" He repeated her words with dead-on mimicry. "My Spanish may not be as good as yours, but trust me, I got the subtext."

Benny looked away. Owen *was* a distraction, and it wasn't just those eyes or the deep set of dimples that accompanied his ready grin. He could walk into a room and she'd find herself tuned like a metal fork against a table. Maybe she couldn't block out that attraction, but she was determined to keep herself committed to her mission.

"I didn't mean to hurt your feelings." It had never

occurred to her that he would notice the absence of one person's adulation. Everybody loved Owen—her supervisors, the children who ran around the village, the visiting medical personnel. Kyle Garrett idolized him. "Anyway, I *know* you can speak Spanish. That's why you're so useful entertaining the kids while they're waiting to be treated." She risked another look at him and found him frowning at the instrument panel. "What's the matter?"

"Uh, we may have a slight problem."

"What do you mean?"

Jaw shifting, he flipped a switch or two. There wasn't a dimple in sight. "Either the fuel gauge is out of commission or both tanks are leaking. Neither's a particularly good scenario."

"You think bullets hit the fuel tanks?"

"Don't know. Hold on, let me see who I can get on the radio. Mayday! Mayday! Broncobuster to control tower…"

Benny sat still as his attention focused on the instrument panel and his headset. He was a skilled pilot with thousands of flight hours under his belt, and she could trust him with her life. The Cessna didn't seem to be losing altitude, but what did *she* know?

Looked like she'd dodged out of one dangerous situation right into another—worse than the guy in the dark suit and tie who'd shown up at the clinic yesterday afternoon. Flashing a badge, he'd asked if he could have a few minutes of her time.

Surrounded by screaming babies, worried mothers and fishermen with rotten teeth, she'd nearly booted him out without apology. But when he'd asked if she knew Celine Andrews, she'd handed the baby in her arms to Stacy Garrett and stepped outside.

How could anybody have connected her to a woman she hadn't seen since she was fifteen years old—and traced her all the way to the Yucatán?

Lord, it's me again. Please help me know what to tell Owen—and give him wisdom and skill to handle this problem with the plane.

She made the mistake of looking out the side window. They had begun to yaw downward and to the right. Nothing but blue ocean below. Her stomach surged. "Owen!"

"Hold on. The radio's messed up. Must've got hit."

"We're dropping!"

"We should have enough fuel to clear the Gulf." Owen winked at her. "Unless you've got your heart set on going for a little swim." He laughed at her expression. "There's a wide-open field a couple of miles inland, north of Veracruz. That's where I'm headed."

"Can't we land at an airport?"

"Too far away. Hang on."

The plane began to buck like a mustang. Owen's full attention returned to the controls. His jaw tightened as he operated the rudder pedals and control column.

Benny's teeth slammed together as the plane took a roller-coaster dip into a pocket of air. She wasn't going to scream again. She *wasn't*. Gripping the armrests, she closed her eyes. The ride became smooth for several seconds, then hit a corrugated patch that made the plane shake like a tambourine.

Oh, God, have mercy on us. You know I don't swim well.

"You praying?"

"Of course I am."

"Just checking. Another few minutes and we're on the ground. Grab those life jackets under your seat just in case."

Could one pass out from hyperventilation? She couldn't remember ever being this frightened—even when the guy in the suit opened fire on her as she was leaving her room early this morning. She fished the life jackets out from under the seats and helped Owen into his. Fastening her own, she reminded herself how far the Lord had brought her. Her life was in His hands, and He could take it or give it back to her.

Your will be done, Lord.

She peeked out the window again at the jade-and-terra-cotta patchwork of coastal landscape below. Owen banked left and the plane stalled as they lost altitude.

"Hey, who knew Mexico had this many trees?" He tensed. "You might not want to look right now."

"Owen! Look out!" Treetops zoomed at the plane.

"Relax." Limbs and leaves scraped the belly of the plane. "You're in the hands of a—"

She screamed as the landing gear came down with a *fwump,* snicking off the tops of a row of cypress trees. The right wingtip whacked into the trunk of a palm tree. Her stomach was somewhere around her eyebrows. The plane wobbled and skated clear of the trees, the wheels jouncing across somebody's cow pasture. Another couple of wild bounces and they were taxiing.

Owen applied the brakes, his muscles bulging with the strain of holding the plane steady on the rocky field. Benny watched his face, mesmerized by the fierce concentration in his narrowed eyes, flared nostrils and tight lips. Then she glanced out the windshield.

They were headed straight for a barn.

TWO

Raymond Briggs tossed his navy suit coat across a chair and pushed the rifle case under the outdoor cantina table. Scowling at the pretty young waitress waiting to take his order, he yanked out another chair and dropped into it. Drowning his frustration in a shot of tequila would have redeemed some of this miserable day. Unfortunately, one did not order alcohol at ten o'clock in the morning in a conservative city like Villahermosa.

"Agua embotellada, por favor," he growled.

The little waitress scurried inside.

Slouching, Briggs unclipped the cell phone from his belt and stared at it. He'd rather face a mountain lion than have to tell his boss he'd let Bernadette Malone slip through his fingers.

How could he have missed that shot? At least once a week, he'd spend a few hours at a practice range so he wouldn't choke under pressure.

He was a professional. Hidden in the thick vegetation on the outskirts of the camp, he'd waited patiently for a chance to catch the missionary alone. With his binoculars trained on her cabin, he'd seen her and another young woman walk toward a long Quonset-like building, which he assumed to be the cafeteria. Thirty minutes later, she'd returned alone and he'd had his chance. He should have been out of there, his mark dead and no one the wiser; he'd had a silencer on the rifle and he was a genius at disappearing.

But the sting of a mosquito had made him twitch, sending the bullet into the cabin wall. Startled, the woman stood there for a split second. Then, just as he reloaded the chamber, she'd darted toward the old Jeep parked by the door.

Ray kicked the gun case at his feet. How was he going to explain the behavior of this crazy young woman? Why would she drive *away* from the other individuals in the camp? Dumbfounded, he'd knelt for precious seconds with the rifle held to his shoulder as the Jeep sped toward the main road. Arrogantly sure of his aim, he hadn't bothered to sabotage her vehicle.

The waitress returned with his bottled water and Ray gave her a few pesos, silently cursing himself, cursing the woman, cursing the humidity that made his shirt stick to his back. By now, he should have been in Cancún enjoying a short vacation before returning to the southwest Tennessee heat.

Thumb on speed dial, he hesitated before dialing the number. The judge was going to go ballistic.

He lined up defenses in his mind like toy soldiers. How could he have known there was a plane sitting on the beach less than five miles away, with a pilot getting ready to take off? Assumptions, as it turned out, had been the source of his every mistake.

Mistakes for which he was going to pay a major price.

His hand clenched around the phone, his thumb pressing the dial button. "Hey, boss." What a relief to get voice mail instead of the powerful pit bull who could put a knot in his stomach with nothing more than silence. "It's me, Briggs. I, uh, I got bad news. The girl got away. I'm not sure how much she knows, but I'm going after her. My plane leaves in an hour. Cell reception's kinda spotty down here, so you may not be able to get me right away. I'll call you when I hit the States. Don't worry. She's as good as dead."

Owen reviewed his options, both of which called for what his mother referred to as bowling language.

He could turn the plane and mow down a couple of cows.

Or he could crash into the barn. The Cessna was sturdy but not indestructible. Mission Aviation Fellowship functioned largely on donations, and it killed Owen to think about how much repairs would cost.

So he'd just have to stop it.

Ramming his feet down on the brake pedals, feeling the aircraft shudder, he held on to the control column for dear life. The crooked, gaping boards of the barn loomed, closer and closer, until he could almost smell the manure and hay.

He braced himself for impact. Benny had thrown her hands over her face, but at least she had stopped screaming.

God, I need help! Come on, come on, please help me stop this plane.

The plane skidded for another heart-stopping second

or two. They rammed into the barn, with the nose of the plane tucked into the open front door. An odd noise crunched in the right wing as it came to rest against the outside wall.

Trembling, Owen stared into the dark recesses of the barn. "Wow. That was close." A couple of chickens squawked.

"We're not dead, are we?" Benny lowered her hands.

"I don't think so. If this is Heaven, I've got issues with the management." He took off his headphones. "Are you okay?"

"Um, yeah." She unfastened her seat belt and took off the life jacket. "Good thing we didn't need these."

Owen grinned. "Remember when we took the de Cristos kids swimming last summer?" Benny had gotten too far away from shore and couldn't dog-paddle back; then when he went after her, she'd nearly drowned him. For such an accomplished lady, Bernadette was a terrible swimmer.

Who also looked great in a swimsuit, even a style pretty much in line with his grandmother's taste.

"I remember." Benny scowled. "You put a fish down my back."

"It was a two-inch minnow, and he was more traumatized than you."

"Oh, so you think fish abuse is funny." Her eyes were twinkling, though, so maybe she was getting over the shock of their forced landing.

"So what do you say we break out of this joint? Find out who this plantation belongs to."

"I don't think I can get my door open."

"Okay, then come this way."

The double-decker Cessna Combi-Bush was designed with the cockpit high above a deep freight compartment. Owen jumped to the ground, turned and reached for Benny's waist. She put her hands on his shoulders and let him set her lightly down.

She frowned a bit when he didn't immediately step back. Boy, she didn't like to be touched. He wondered if more than water panic had been behind that scene at the river last summer. She'd fought him like a wildcat, even when they were safely in shallow water.

Suddenly, something bumped the back of his legs hard enough to buckle his knees.

"Mba-a-aaa!"

Owen looked down to find a small gray goat backing up to butt him again. "Hey!" He dodged, pulling Benny with him.

She laughed. "We invaded the earthling's territory."

"Looks like." Owen danced to avoid another thrust of the underdeveloped horns.

Benny didn't seem concerned. Standing in a shaft of dusty sunlight, she absently reached down to pet the animal's nappy head as she surveyed their surroundings. "How're we gonna get out of here? The plane's blocking the door."

"I'm surprised we didn't knock the whole barn down." Owen looked up to examine the tin roof. It was apparently sturdier than it appeared.

"Look, there are a bunch of loose boards over here." Bernadette walked over to the corner and started shoving at the walls.

"Watch out! You'll have the place falling on our heads." Owen followed her and saw that she was right.

With one good kick, he could open a space big enough for them to slip through. "Stand back, I'm gonna—"

"*¿Quién está?*" demanded someone outside the barn. "*¡Voy a disparar!*"

Benny's big dark eyes widened. "Did he just say he'd shoot us?" She peered through a knothole in the wall and said in Spanish, "Please, señor, we're Americans! We had to make an emergency landing, but we won't hurt you. Can you get us out of here?"

The voice growled out a series of Spanish words. Then the boards in front of them began to splinter and fall away from the outside. Owen and Benny found themselves staring into the myopic brown eyes of an elderly Mexican gentleman carrying an equally ancient shotgun. He had apparently used it to pry loose the wall.

"You are scaring my chickens," he said in surly Spanish, moving back so Benny could squeeze through the narrow opening. "I should charge you a hundred pesos' compensation."

"Reckon he's gonna send 'em to poultry therapy?" Owen sucked in his breath to follow Benny.

She gave him a quelling look, then batted her long, curly lashes at the farmer. "We are so sorry for the inconvenience." She glanced at the plane, stuck in the doorway of the barn for all the world like an alien spacecraft in an Ed Wood movie. "We've got a problem with the fuel tanks, and one of the wings is broken. We can't move it right now. If you would be so kind as to let us leave it here until we can have someone come repair it, we'll be glad to pay you a storage fee."

"How am I supposed to get in to feed my animals?" The farmer folded his skinny arms without lowering the gun.

Owen decided he'd been quiet long enough. "You've got a nice new opening started right here. I'll help you straighten it up and build a door."

"I won't pay you one peso." The farmer's gaze fell on Benny's face and softened. "However, my wife will give you a good dinner before you—" he glared at Owen "—go away."

Owen had no desire to impose himself on the farmer's dubious hospitality any longer than absolutely necessary. He pulled Bernadette aside.

"The least I can do is repair the old guy's chicken coop. While I'm doing that, why don't you sweet-talk him into giving us directions to Poza Rica?"

"But that's a big city. I think we should avoid crowds. We need to go around—"

"All right, all right. I'll let you make that call. But sooner or later, we *are* going to talk." He searched her face. Avoiding his eyes, she stood there with arms folded and one toe drawing circles in the dirt. Owen had never had any patience for puzzles. "Benny—"

"Okay, Owen." She sighed. "I owe you an explanation. But not now." She glanced at the farmer, whose gray brows beetled in patent suspicion. "You fix the door and I'll see if I can come up with some other mode of transportation."

Benny turned her beautiful smile on the farmer, who unbent enough to lower the muzzle of the gun to the ground. With Benny jabbering in enthusiastic Spanish, the two of them headed toward a small adobe house sitting on a lumpy hill about a hundred yards away.

Owen slipped back into the barn and climbed into the cockpit of the plane. Benny wouldn't like it, but he was going to try the radio again. They'd taken off without filing a flight plan and he had to let somebody know what had happened. Otherwise, people were going to worry.

His brother, for example. Eli was a Border Patrol agent, too, and hadn't been wild about Owen taking this little jaunt. The prototypical big brother, Eli had become a total worrywart since a month ago, when he'd taken on a wife and a couple of kids.

As if flying medical supplies across the Gulf of Mexico was any more dangerous than chasing illegal aliens and dope peddlers through the desert.

Settling into his seat and adjusting the headphones, Owen paused in the act of flipping the radio on. Come to think of it, things *had* turned a little dicey in the last few hours.

Oh, well. Eli would just have to get over it.

After supper, Benny sat beside her hostess on the sagging sofa in the family room, where the only light came from an oil lamp and a string of multicolored Christmas bulbs strung along the ceiling. Mariela, a tiny butterball of a woman distinguished by a gray-streaked black bun and an enormous wart on the side of her nose, had given them coffee and empanadas for dessert.

Benny wished she'd had a video camera to record Owen dealing with Gustavo and Mariela de Oca. Over a simple meal taken at their kitchen table, Owen had piled on lavish praise for the good señora's frijoles and tamales until she wouldn't hear of her guests continuing their odyssey without a good night's sleep. Furthermore, he'd apparently done such a good job with the barn door that even crusty old Gustavo was ready to apply for membership in the Owen Carmichael fan club.

Trying not to wince as she sipped the strong coffee, Benny watched Owen playing *el juego de damas*— checkers—on the bottom of a cardboard box with their host. Gustavo sat cross-legged on the tile floor, while Owen reclined on his side, his long legs taking up most of the floor space. He could make himself at home in any situation. He'd make a wonderful missionary.

"Your husband is a handsome young man." Mariela straightened her flowered housedress. "You have been married for long?"

Benny choked and wiped coffee off her skirt. "He's not my husband."

Mariela frowned. "But you travel together without a chaperone?"

How wonderful to meet a lady with scruples as antiquated as her own. "We're traveling together sort of by accident. We'd planned to reach our destination before dark. I'm happy you and Gustavo can be our chaperones."

Mariela pursed her lips. "For one night. What will you do after that?"

Benny shrugged. "Owen's a gentleman. I never have to worry about him." She lifted the coffee cup to shield her face but couldn't help glancing at Owen. There was something powerful and magnetic about the way he'd looked at her while he was in Agrexco this week. His usual teasing expression had been thoughtful. As if he saw into her thoughts and feelings.

Thoughts and feelings she hid pretty carefully. After all, she wanted to present an impression of a godly young Christian woman. Which was, of course, exactly what she was.

Lord, with Your help, I've escaped so much tragedy, she thought as she watched Owen jump three of Gustavo's black checkers. *Why? Why let that man stir it up again?* So many men in her life had sent her down destructive paths. She couldn't help lining Owen up with the lot of them, measuring to see how he fit.

He suddenly grinned at something Gustavo said and Benny hastily dropped her gaze to watch him jingling a handful of checkers. He had beautiful hands—long, deft fingers with neatly trimmed nails—and he wore a big college class ring with a blue stone on his right hand. She noticed a gash across his thumb, probably from his impromptu carpentry work that afternoon. He could do pretty much anything that came his way.

She stood up. "Owen, is there a first aid kit in the plane?"

"Sure, it's in the cockpit, in the compartment between the—hey, where are you going?"

"Your thumb's bleeding." She handed her coffee cup to Mariela, who blinked in surprise. "I'll be right back."

Owen caught up to her as she pushed open the screen door. "I don't want you going out there by yourself."

She paused, wishing he'd stayed put but not entirely surprised that he hadn't. "Why not?"

"Because it's dark. And…there's a killer goat out there."

"Ooh. You're gonna protect me from the big bad baby goat?" She patted her chest as if overcome. Owen grinned and she smiled. "Look, Mariela already thinks we're into scandalous behavior. We need to be careful."

His eyes narrowed. "Good grief. What a busybody."

Benny shrugged. "She asked if we were married. When I told her no, she assumed... Well, I said I was glad for her to chaperone." She looked up at Owen, relieved to have this discussion out in the open. She didn't want any misunderstandings. "Listen, Owen, my credibility as a single female missionary hinges on my reputation. I've got to make sure we're not alone at night. Ever."

He stared back at her, his jaw shifting. "Okay. I guess I can see that. But for the record, you know I'd never... you know you can trust me, right?"

She weighed her words carefully. "I don't think you'd do anything on purpose, but..." She sighed. "Well, I know when a man is looking at me a certain way."

His mouth opened and she fully expected him to blast her for her conceit, but then his gaze unexpectedly wavered. "There's nothing wrong with looking at a beautiful woman," he muttered.

Benny couldn't help the little thrill of pleasure his words—and his confused expression—sent through her midsection. *Oh, Lord, forgive me. I thought I was past that hunger for approval....*

She crossed her arms over her stomach. "That's very sweet of you to say that, but I really need you to help me be...circumspect. Do you know what I mean?"

She had to endure the intense blue-green gaze scanning her face, touching her lips. Finally, he smiled a little. "No looking, huh?"

She shook her head. "And we've been in here by ourselves long enough. Go play checkers with Gustavo

and I'll get the first aid kit. I can't have my pilot coming
down with gangrene."

"Yeah, that would be inconvenient." Owen pushed
away from the doorjamb. Placing his hands over his
eyes, he backed away. "Just call me See No Evil."

Benny laughed and headed out into the moonlit yard.
A flashlight would have been nice, but they'd left that
in the plane, too, along with Owen's luggage and some
stuff the Garretts had sent back to the States. Benny
herself had no personal items whatsoever. She'd left in
such a panic she hadn't even had time to grab her purse.

She shuddered, remembering the zip of the bullet
whizzing over her head to plant itself in the concrete
wall behind her. Had it really happened less than
twenty-four hours ago?

Now she had no cash, no credit cards, no ID, no
phone—nothing but the clothes on her back. Getting
safely across Mexico was going to stretch her faith and
intellect to the limit.

Owen Carmichael would never have been her first
choice of escorts. *Lord, why not somebody safe? Somebody a little less…charismatic?*

Pushing open the barn door that Owen had created
from the boards he'd cut out of the wall, Benny poked
her head inside. She could hear the animals rustling in
their stalls. She wasn't afraid of the little goat, but the
idea of getting butted in the dark didn't appeal, either.
Hopefully he was locked in a stall for the night.

If the barn had been shadowy in the daytime, it was
positively Cimmerian tonight, and it smelled like…well,
like a barn. A draft through the open door stirred the hay
and she sneezed. Leaving the door open so the moon-

light could filter in, she waited a moment until her eyes adjusted to the darkness. As hangars went, this one was on the cramped side. The nose of the plane loomed over her head to the left and she could barely discern the outline of the door panel in front of the wings.

A moment later, she had the door open and managed to lower the steps. By the glow of the interior light, she climbed into the cabin. Sliding into the pilot's seat, she laid her head back against the soft leather back of the chair. Astonishing, this sudden feeling of being enveloped by Owen. Even more surprising was the realization that she didn't feel threatened. Just safe.

She studied the instrument panel. Earlier in the day, she'd been too frightened to pay much attention to all those dials, knobs and switches. Clearly it would take a pretty good brain to operate a million-dollar aircraft like this. Owen liked to perpetrate a class-clown persona, but he had hidden depths. *Well* hidden.

She grinned to herself. Okay, the first aid kit. He said it would be in the compartment between the seats. She lifted the lid of the box, which reached to about the level of the armrests. Its interior light revealed a couple of maps, a pair of sunglasses and a spiral-bound notebook. She dumped them all in her lap to continue digging for the first aid kit.

There it was, a white metal box with the traditional red cross on top. She opened it and removed the antibiotic ointment, as well as a couple of adhesive bandages, then put the box back in the bottom of the compartment.

She examined Owen's aviator sunglasses before returning them to the console. Expensive. Quality eyewear must be a necessity for a pilot. She started to put the remaining two items in her lap back into the console when a photograph fell out of the notebook and slipped to the floor. Sticking the maps in a niche beside Owen's sunglasses, she reached down to pick up the picture.

She turned it over and caught her breath. "Oh, my…."

It was a snapshot taken the day of the swimming expedition. She'd let a couple of the little girls bury her feet in the sand and Owen had captured her close-up, with her head thrown back, laughing.

He was quite a good amateur photographer, and he'd shown her the other pictures he'd taken of the children that day. But she hadn't imagined he would stick this one in a notebook and bring it all the way to Mexico.

Her heart thumped a little. Just how deeply engaged were his feelings for her?

THREE

Chief Justice of the Tennessee Supreme Court, the Honorable J. Paul Grenville III, had pulled his Harley into one of the historic roadside parks along I-20 to Memphis. He sat on a picnic table with his cell phone pressed to his ear. On his way home from Nashville for the weekend, he'd stopped to check up on a certain international project.

"What do you mean, you missed her?" In his agitation, he dropped his helmet and it went bouncing against some Confederate soldier's headstone. Probably one of Grenville's ancestors. He was related to half the state of Tennessee.

The voice on the other end of the cell connection surged and dropped out. What good was the North American Free Trade Agreement when you couldn't even get a good cell connection with employees in Mexico?

"—didn't get close enough for a clear shot," he finally heard. "They took off, headed across the Gulf."

"Took off? You mean in a boat?"

"No! Some big blond guy had a Cessna freight plane parked on the beach. There was a kid there, too, but he drove off in the girl's Jeep before I got close."

"You checked out the plane, right? Where did it go?" Grenville picked up his helmet and paced along the concrete sidewalk edging the cemetery. Briggs had been in his employ for nearly twenty years, since the days when Grenville had been on the Tennessee Court of Appeals. Briggs was methodical, thorough and ruthless. In a word, invaluable.

"Of course I did. Turns out he's an off-duty Border Patrol agent on a supply run for some missionary outfit out of Laredo. I figure that's where they're heading."

"Make sure." Grenville mounted the bike. "Get the flight plan and intercept them when they land. It would have been a lot easier to get her before she reached the States."

"I know." Briggs made a disgusted noise. "She really fooled me during the interview. I thought I had the wrong woman until I poked through her stuff while she was out of the room."

"You better get something straight right now, Briggs. This girl is young, but she is not stupid." In fact, that had been the thing that most attracted Grenville once upon a time. "I'm counting on you to keep her from scotching this appointment."

"You know I will, sir."

"And Briggs—"

"Yes, sir?"

"The pilot has to go, too."

Grenville ended the call and sat there a moment, contemplating the budding greenery in the woods behind the cemetery. He had sacrificed too much to let some little ex-hooker ruin his chances at one of the most powerful posts in the judicial branch of government.

* * *

Gustavo snored like a B-52 bomber, and Owen woke up with a crick in his neck from trying to keep his ears covered while sleeping on a tile floor with nothing but his arm for a pillow. He and Eli had camped all their lives, so roughing it wasn't a problem. Still, he'd found himself tossing and turning all night.

The look on Bernadette's face when she'd come in, armed with ointment and Band-Aids, would probably give him nightmares for months. Demanding to see his thumb, she'd squirted half a tube of medicine on him and nearly cut off his circulation with a bandage. Then she'd disappeared behind the curtain, where she and Señora de Oca would sleep.

He couldn't understand her sudden agitation. After the crash landing, she seemed to have settled down, almost enjoying the impromptu bed-and-breakfast scenario. Maybe she was worrying about whoever had shot at her in Agrexco. One way or another, he was gonna have to find out what that was all about.

He sat up, stretching, and looked at the backlit dial of his watch. Not quite 5:00 a.m. and Gustavo was already gone, apparently outside tending to his animals. Maybe there would be eggs for breakfast.

There wasn't much light yet in the dingy little living room; Mariela had unplugged the Christmas bulbs before following Benny to bed, and the sun barely glowed around the edges of the thick polyester curtains hanging in the windows. Owen had a sudden overwhelming urge to get out of this place. He'd have been happier spending the night in the plane, but leaving Benny alone wasn't an option. Though Mariela and Gustavo de Oca seemed like nice enough people, he felt better knowing Benny was just on the other side of that curtain.

Pulling on his boots, he wondered if she'd slept well. *No looking,* he reminded himself as he glanced at the curtain. He quietly let himself out the kitchen door.

He walked down the hill toward the barn, intending to inspect the plane before Benny got up and around. A thorough examination revealed that, besides the holes in the fuel tanks, which he could have patched, the right wing had a long crack near the fuselage. Without the tools or materials to fix it, he felt like a surgeon diagnosing an inoperable tumor.

Getting Benny safely home in a reasonable amount of time was going to be a challenge. He didn't have much cash, and the border was a long way off. Laying a hand on the cool steel belly of the aircraft, he spent a few minutes praying for wisdom.

Feeling immeasurably stronger, he went searching for old Gustavo and found him inside the barn, feeding the goat. The little billy gave Owen a disdainful bleat, then went back to his hay.

"Good morning, Gustavo." Owen leaned over the top of the stall. "Thanks for your hospitality."

"It's nothing." Gustavo propped his hands atop his pitchfork. "We don't see many Americans out here, so you must excuse my rudeness yesterday. I thought you might be drug traffickers running from the law."

Owen smiled at the irony of that remark. "Not a chance. Do you have any idea where we might get hold of a car?"

"Now *that,*" Gustavo said, "is a large problem. As I told the señorita last night, all I have is my truck, and my closest neighbor is twenty kilometers away. Unless—"

he scratched his whiskery chin "—unless you want to ride my mule up to Poza Rica. My cousin Jorge runs a used-car lot and I'm sure he'd give you a good deal."

Owen thought of several objections to that plan, not least of which was Benny's desire to stay away from cities. Still, their choices were limited. "Couldn't *you* drive Benny and me to Poza Rica? We'd be glad to pay you—"

But Gustavo was shaking his head. "I'm sorry, but I can't leave right now. Lajuana is due to drop her calf. She had trouble last time."

Having grown up around horses, Owen understood the concept of protecting one's livestock. Still, the prospect of riding a mule twenty miles struck him as a bit over the top. "But won't you need your mule?"

"It is only mid-March." Gustavo shrugged. "I won't plow for another two weeks, at least. You could leave Sunflower with Jorge. I will drive up to get him later."

"Okay, then, how about letting us *borrow* your truck? I'll pay someone to drive it back to you. The plane's good collateral, don't you think?"

"I need my truck." Gustavo picked up the pitchfork and went back to work, the subject obviously closed. "If you don't want to take Sunflower, you can walk."

Owen glanced over his shoulder at the busted-up plane, then at the swaybacked mule, contentedly munching oats in its stall a few feet away.

Oh, how the mighty are fallen.

Benny was scrambling eggs on Mariela's ancient stove when Owen came in the back door, carrying a bucket of milk. He plunked it on the table and walked up behind her. "I was hoping somebody would have breakfast going. That smells good."

She glanced over her shoulder. With golden-brown bristle covering his jaw and a sleepy droop at the corners of his eyes, he looked a little worse for wear. "Where have you been?"

"Negotiating a deal with Gustavo." He reached over her shoulder and snitched a strip of bacon.

"What kind of deal?"

He leaned on the counter and licked grease off his fingers. "Let's just say I didn't get the better end of it. More specifically, my *end* may wind up whooped."

Benny had to giggle. "That sounds ominous."

"I'll say. Old Gustavo wouldn't part with his truck, so it looks like Sunflower and I will be taking a little field trip."

"Sunflower? Who's that?"

"Not *who—it.* Sunflower's a mule, my transportation to Poza Rica. I'll ride up there, buy a car from Gustavo's cousin Jorge and come back to get you."

Benny stared at him. He looked perfectly serious. "You're not leaving me here."

He cocked his head. "Benny, I shouldn't be gone more than a day—two at the most. Mariela will take good care of—"

"No, I'll go with you. That will save time."

Owen's blue-green eyes lost their sleepy look. "What are you afraid of? You know we lost the guy in the Land Rover. There's no way he could catch up to us."

"They'll know we never made it to Laredo. Anybody can look up a flight plan." Shivering, Benny turned off the stove and shoved the pan full of eggs off the burner.

"I didn't have time to file a flight plan." Owen took her by the shoulders when she would have turned away. "Bernadette, who's after you? Is it more than just this one man?"

She stood stiff under his hands and looked at the strong brown column of his throat. "I'm not sure."

"This is insane." Frustration laced his voice. "How can I protect you—and myself, for that matter—if I don't know what we're running from?"

He was right. It wasn't fair to keep Owen in the dark, but if she told him about Paul Grenville, Grenville would do his best to kill Owen, too. On the other hand, she refused to lie.

She made herself relax. "Okay, you're right. It's silly to worry like this. Go ahead and take the mule to Poza Rica."

Several seconds ticked by. Benny felt Owen's big, gentle hands tighten, the thumbs on her collarbones and palms cupping her shoulders. When she looked up at him his expression speared her to the heart.

"You'll be gone when I get back, won't you?" His lips pressed together as he let her go. "I can't believe you have so little regard for me."

Benny caught her balance against the table. "Owen, you don't understand who these people are. I care for you too much to let you—"

"You care for me?" Owen uttered a harsh laugh, the kind she'd never imagined him capable of. "Then trust me with the truth."

She put her hands to her face and closed her eyes. "Okay, listen. Here's all I can tell you now. When I was very young, I had some bad experiences and they've come back to haunt me. I have to get to Memphis to see an old friend, find out what she knows."

After another moment's silence, Owen sighed. "Why not call her?"

"We've just been in touch by e-mail because I'm afraid my calls can be traced. I have to see her in person."

"Memphis," Owen muttered. "I thought we were going to Laredo."

Benny lowered her hands. "Will you help me get back to the States? Without asking questions?"

He shook his head. "You are a crazy woman, you know that?"

"I know. Please, Owen?"

"Like I could ever say no to you." It wasn't a question.

After breakfast, Owen saddled Sunflower with Gustavo's old-fashioned tack, then mounted the mule with the confidence of long practice. Getting Benny situated was a bit trickier.

At least he'd talked her into trading in her full, flowery skirt for his extra pair of jeans.

"Come on, Ben," he'd teased, "you'll have saddle sores on your saddle sores if you try to ride in a skirt."

So she'd rolled up the legs three or four times and tied them at the waist with a leather strap Gustavo had lying around the barn. She actually looked pretty cute, in a countrified kind of way.

"Okay, now stand over on the left side of the mule— watch out! He'll kick if you get too close to his rear." Owen was sweating already; he could just imagine what the heat would be like this afternoon. He'd give anything for his straw cowboy hat or even his Border Patrol headgear.

Benny looked up at him, hands on hips. "How'm I going to get up there?"

He extended his left hand. "Okay, put your left foot— no, your *other* left foot," he said with a grin "—in the stirrup. That's it. Now grab my wrist with both hands and I'll pull you up. Hang on. Here you go!"

She swung up easily, fitting neatly behind the deep, old-fashioned cantle of the saddle.

"I did it!"

"Good girl. Now give my stirrup back and hold on." When she clutched the sides of his shirt, he looked over his shoulder. "You're gonna have to get a little more aggressive than that."

"I'll be fine."

"Whatever you say," he said with a little smile and a shrug. Waving at Gustavo and Mariela, who stood at the kitchen door watching the show, he kicked Sunflower lightly in the ribs. "Yippee-ki-yo!"

As Owen had anticipated, the mule's gait would have registered about 5.0 on the Richter scale. Benny was forced to hang on for dear life.

The mule also expressed, at regular intervals, noisy objection to his double load, which kept their conversation to a minimum. Since Owen had nothing to do but keep Sunflower from turning around to head back to the barn, he passed the time mulling over this morning's conversation with Benny.

Bad experiences when she was very young. What did that mean? Most people he knew had traumatic experiences of one kind or another. He could never understand people who let tragedy dictate their lives. Owen figured you could make your own sunshine.

Not that Benny seemed to dwell on negative things as a rule. He'd always observed her to be a can-do person. She'd tackled issues with a Mexican orphanage that would have made most women run screaming back to the good old U.S. of A.

Now here she was, mounted behind him like Calamity Jane, arms wrapped around his waist and heels bouncing in rhythm with Sunflower's bone-jarring trot. Wondering what she was thinking, he looked down at her slim hands, clasped under his rib cage. Her skin was the color of coffee with cream, her nails short and unpolished but beautifully groomed. She had a little silver ring with a turquoise stone on her right pinkie, and her watch—a simple bangle—was silver as well.

He took an experimental breath, filling his lungs to make Benny's arms tighten around him. Sunflower seemed to have settled down. "You okay back there?"

"J-just peachy. How much longer 'til we get there?"

"About five more hours."

"Five *hours?*" Owen felt a gusty sigh against his back. "I thought I was in pretty good shape, but I'm beginning to feel muscles I didn't know I had."

"Wait 'til you try to get to sleep tonight."

"Oh, thanks. You're such an encouragement. I guess this is no big deal for you, huh?"

"Well, old Sunflower's not exactly in the same league as my cutting horse."

"You ride the rodeo circuit?"

"Yup. Three-time amateur calf-roping regional champ. Got the buckles to prove it."

Bernadette chuckled. "I'd like to see you ride sometime."

Owen felt his chest swell a bit. "You could come this fall, after you get home."

There was a short silence. "I'm not sure where home is."

"I'm guessing Mexico doesn't cut it."

"Not yet."

"Is Memphis your stomping ground?"

"No." He thought she wasn't going to elaborate, but then she said, "I grew up in Collierville. It's a little bit east of Memphis."

"Really? Tell me about your family. You got brothers and sisters?"

"No, I was in foster care."

"Oh." Kids in foster care generally came from messed-up families that they'd just as soon you didn't mention. *Bad experiences.*

He briefly laid his hand on top of hers and felt her fingers flutter against his palm. "I'm sorry, Benny."

"One of my foster moms gave me a Bible. She was a nice lady."

Owen didn't find it nearly as easy to talk about spiritual things as his brother did, but he couldn't pass up the opportunity to get Benny to talk. "Is she the one who taught you about the Lord?"

"She tried. Her name was Mrs. Coker. How about you? How did you come to know Christ?"

"The usual. Vacation Bible school. Mom had us in church every time the doors were open."

"You're very blessed, Owen."

"I know." He shifted in the saddle. "But then my dad blew it all at the end. I don't understand how he could throw our family away for money. I always looked up to him as a kid. He was my hero."

Three years ago Owen's father, a Border Patrol agent, had been involved in a smuggling scheme that had resulted in the murder of two other agents. A year later he'd been killed while trying to cover his tracks. Owen's mother was just now getting over the tragedy.

Benny was quiet for a moment. Then to Owen's astonishment she laced her fingers through his. "Lots of times people self-destruct when they're separated from God, Owen. Make sure you stay close to Him."

Owen could have sworn she laid her cheek against his back for a fleeting second. He decided it must have been his imagination.

Still, he was strangely comforted, even when Benny released his hand and began to sing, off-key, *"Arroz con leche."*

Rice pudding, huh? He goosed Sunflower with his heels. Poza Rica was a long way off.

"Wait a minute, Briggs." Grenville turned off the speakerphone and shut the door of his home office. He sank back into the antique leather chair and swiveled to face the picture window looking out onto his front lawn. "What did you find out?"

"They didn't make it to Laredo."

"Then where did they go?"

"Seems they made an emergency landing somewhere

north of Veracruz. Some farmers in the area reported it. I must have nicked the fuel tanks."

Grenville watched two hummingbirds squabbling over the red glass feeder hanging from the eaves. He found their antics soothing. "Where are you now?"

"Laredo, their intended destination."

"Then you'll just have to backtrack. Head for the area where the plane turned up."

Briggs sighed. "I'm on it."

"Briggs…" Grenville paused, picking up the morning newspaper covering his desk blotter. The front page of the editorial section displayed an old file photo of himself, sharing a basketball trophy with his college roommate and cocaptain—now the President of the United States.

"Yeah, boss?"

Grenville tossed the paper into the trash can. "Find them."

FOUR

Benny slid off the mule and into Owen's arms. Her thigh muscles ached, her knees were rubbery and there were blisters in places she didn't want to think about. To make it worse, her stomach had been rumbling for the last hour. It was past noon and Owen had to be starving, too.

Owen grabbed the mule's harness. "Are you okay?"

"Fine, thanks." She stepped back, staggering a little. "I'll get out lunch while you take care of Sunflower."

They'd stopped at a small pond just off the dusty, rutted track they'd been following for the last two hours. The sight of the little brown pool had instantly centered Benny's misery on her parched mouth and throat. *Water. Blessed gift of a good God.*

She unbuckled the saddle pack, keeping a wary eye on Sunflower's broad hindquarters. She extracted a couple of bottles of water they'd brought from the plane and the burritos Mariela had sent. Owen ground-tied the mule, letting it graze on the weeds at the edge of the pond.

Benny handed Owen a bottle of water, smiling when he twisted off the cap and glugged it down in one long swallow.

He wiped his mouth with the back of his hand. "Wish we didn't have to leave the other two cases back in the plane."

"I know, but Gustavo and Mariela will enjoy it. We owed them a little something for their trouble."

"You mean besides a new door in their barn?" Owen's mouth quirked as he put the empty plastic bottle back in the saddle pack. He accepted one of the newspaper-wrapped rolls in Benny's hand. "What's on the menu?"

"Burritos."

Owen grimaced. He sat down in the skimpy shade of a mesquite tree near the pond and opened the packet. "Burritos for breakfast, burritos for lunch, burritos for supper. I'm beginning to sympathize with the Israelites' manna complex."

"At least Mariela's a good cook and her kitchen was clean." Too sore to sit, Benny leaned against the tree and ate where she stood. Biting into the soft flour tortilla, she found it filled with spicy rice, beans and a trace of chicken. "Mmm…I should've gotten the recipe."

Owen lifted his sunglasses and squinted at her, eyes inhumanly blue-green in the bright noonday sun. "You're kidding, right?"

She shrugged. "I like to cook. Rolling tortillas is an art."

"Ever since I've known you, you've been busy taking care of orphans and translating for medical teams. When do you ever have time to cook?"

Benny smiled. "Granted, Rosie did most of the cooking at the orphanage, but I had to help. I learned when I was in high school."

"Oh." Sliding his glasses onto the top of his blond

head, Owen swallowed the last of his burrito. "Sit down, kid, you're makin' me noivous."

Laughing, Benny gingerly sat down and stretched out her legs. "Ooh, you were right about the saddle sores."

Wearing pants again felt strange. Hot and itchy. At least it was a modest outfit, and she should be grateful Owen had let her borrow them. He had on lightweight cargo shorts and a white Promise Keepers T-shirt. He'd shoved the sleeves up onto his shoulders and she couldn't keep her eyes off the hard brown biceps that flexed and rolled every time he moved.

"So who taught you? Mrs. Coker?"

"Huh?" Benny jerked her gaze to Owen's face.

He wadded the newspaper that had wrapped his meal. "Who taught you to cook? You said Mrs. Coker was one of your foster mothers."

Food, Benny. He's talking about food. "No, Mrs. Coker was from my Tennessee days, before—" She snapped her jaws together. "I moved to south Mississippi and finished high school with the Gonzales family." Rattled, she forced a smile. "Miss Roxanne was my culinary coach. You should try my chicken and dumplings."

"Believe me, I'd love to." Owen canted his head, fixing her with his deceptively sleepy gaze. "I bet you have lots of unsuspected talents."

She stared at him, heat rising to her cheeks. He didn't mean anything by that. He didn't know. He *couldn't* know. And even if he did, he'd never deliberately insult her. "Well, I speak fluent Hebrew," she said lightly. "That's always useful."

Owen let out a crack of laughter. "How come you decided to study that language?"

She shrugged, offering him the last of her burrito, which he swallowed in one bite. "I did my graduate work in missions, but my Hebrew-studies class hooked me, so I decided to stick around for a Ph.D."

He looked at her openmouthed for a moment. "How old are you, Bernadette?"

"You're not supposed to ask a lady her age."

"Since you look like you're about sixteen, that's hardly an insulting question. Come on, how old?"

Benny pulled her legs up and wrapped her arms around her knees. "Twenty-seven."

"And you've been in Mexico for over a year. What are you, a genius? Nobody gets a Ph.D. at the age of twenty-six."

"People do it all the time. I graduated from Delta State at twenty-one and went straight to seminary." Benny ducked her head. "I'm...very focused."

"Yeah, right." Owen snorted. "That's what *I'd* call it. Why did I not know this about you?"

"Well, the subject just doesn't come up in everyday conversation." Back home in Del Rio/Acuña, Owen and his older brother, Eli, had often come to the orphanage to deliver supplies or take the older kids on outings. Benny had appreciated the help, but there never was much time for adult fellowship. Even at church, she'd deliberately kept Owen at arm's length. Male-female relationships were a complication she didn't need or want.

Now... Well, there was nobody around but her, Owen and Sunflower. She could hardly refuse to talk to him. That would just make him more curious.

Her glance fell on his big college ring. "Where did

you go to college?" Men always loved to talk about themselves.

He held up the ring, which glinted in the sunlight. "Baylor. Class of two thousand."

"Really? What did you study?"

"Criminal justice. Then I went to Border Patrol Academy and came back to Texas." He looked a bit sheepish. "I'm kind of a homebody."

Benny rested her chin on her knees and studied him. She'd always been a rootless person, self-contained and lonely. Owen, on the other hand, was deeply attached to his family and his home in Del Rio. Self-confident, recklessly extroverted and full of fun and adventure, he never met a stranger and had a talent for turning adversaries into allies. She deeply admired him.

And secretly feared him.

"Well, Mr. Homebody, if we're going to make it back to the States sometime this year, we'd better hit the road. We have to get to Poza Rica before Gustavo's cousin closes his car lot." She pushed herself to her feet, starting a little when Owen took her elbow to help her up. "Thanks." She forced herself not to jerk away from his hand. She had to keep reminding herself that Owen was a gentleman. *He's not grabbing you, Benny. Chill.*

Old habits were hard to break.

On the outskirts of Poza Rica, Owen and Benny were stopped by a gun-toting *federal* sitting just off the road in a rusty blue truck that looked like it had been hauling chickens since the Nixon era. The officer got out and gestured for them to dismount.

"*¿Drogas?*" He pointed to the saddlebags.

Owen grabbed Sunflower's halter to keep him from taking another nip at the officer's black T-shirt sleeve. *"¡No drogas!"* That was all they needed—to get hauled off to the Mexican pokey, accused of transporting drugs. He would have given anything to be able to flash a U.S. Border Patrol badge and ease on down the road.

Instead he opened the saddlebags and let the *federal* paw through them.

Owen's experience with the Mexican national police force had been mixed. Just last year he and Eli had worked closely with an undercover officer named Artemio Petrarca in an operation to rescue Eli's wife from a brutal smuggler, kidnapper and murderer. Artemio was a fine policeman. But in other quarters Owen had encountered graft, corruption and downright laziness. He hoped this guy would belong to the former category.

Judging by the way his and Bernadette's stuff was getting strewn all over the side of the road, though, they were about to experience a good old Mexican *mordedura,* or "bite."

The officer eyed Benny in a way that made Owen want to clock him. *"Déme cincuenta dólares."*

"Fifty dollars?" Owen let go of the harness. Sunflower could have at the guy.

"¿Porqué?" Why? Benny coolly folded her arms.

No Mexican officer would argue directly with a woman if there was a man nearby. The *federal* flicked a glance at her, then turned to Owen. *"Cincuenta dólares,"* he repeated. *"Por el peaje."*

Sunflower was straddling a pothole the size of a small car and the guy wanted them to pay a toll? Clearly they weren't going to get away without a donation to the *federal*'s bank account.

Owen hid a grin and pretended to think. *"Cinco,"* he finally offered. Five.

"¿Cinco?" The officer frowned, shaking his head. *"Treinta."* Thirty.

"Siete." Owen ignored Benny's squeak of protest. Seven bucks ought to be enough to get rid of the guy.

Scowling, the officer put his hand on his gun. *"Diez."*

"Owen—" Benny grabbed his arm "—give him the money so we can get out of here."

He stared down at her for a moment, startled by the real fear in her eyes. Maybe she had a point. The guy would remember two Anglos giving him such a hard time. Making himself relax, he reached for his wallet, which contained nine American dollars. He handed it all to the officer. *"No tengo más."* I don't have any more.

Except the three hundred-dollar bills he'd stashed in one of his shoes.

The *federal* glared for a few seconds, which wasn't too intimidating since Owen towered over the guy by at least a foot. Finally the man stepped back, waving Owen and Benny on. *"Salgan ustedes."* Get out of here. He muttered a few choice phrases about cheap tourists.

For Benny's sake, Owen ignored him and swung onto the mule's back. Hoisting Benny up behind him, he kicked their intrepid steed into motion. He could feel the *federal*'s stare as they trotted down the road.

When they were out of earshot, Benny sighed against his back. "I hope he doesn't have a radio."

"Yeah. If somebody's looking for us, he won't have any problem describing us."

"Owen, we're going to have to split up. I'm the one they want and I can easily make it back to the States by myself. With my coloring I can pass for Hispanic."

"I'm not leaving you to travel through Mexico by yourself." The very idea made Owen's blood pressure rise.

She patted his hand. "You're such a gentleman, but I've been taking care of myself for a long time. I've traveled to other foreign countries alone, my Spanish is fluent and I'm familiar with the culture. I'll really be safer without—"

"No, you would *not* be safer without me!" Owen reined in so hard the mule brayed in protest.

By now they had reached the outer edges of Poza Rica, named "rich hole" because it was Mexico's largest oil town. Derricks rose like skeletal trees in the eastern distance and the Sierra Madre rippled off to the west. In front of them, the buildings of downtown fell into a pile like blocks dumped out of a toy box. Close by, straggling rows of plywood-and-palm-frond shacks stuck out from the road, intersected by sagging power lines. Children played in the junky, flower-bedecked yards, and old men lounged on cars and trucks parked along the dirt streets.

Mexico in its essence. Not particularly frightening at first glance. But all kinds of danger lay in wait for an unaccompanied woman.

He hooked a leg over the old-fashioned saddle horn and turned sideways. He could see the fragile violet veins at her temples, and long, curly black wisps had come loose from her braid to blow against his cheek. Beautiful and vulnerable.

"Okay, lady, let's have this out once and for all. You claim to be so good at interpreting men. Did you not see the way that *federal* was looking at you?" He leaned in, practically nose to nose. "You. Are. Stuck. With. Me. Period."

She stared up at him, mouth pursed to protest. Then something shifted in her expression and she looked away. "I guess I shouldn't expect you to say anything else." She didn't exactly sound grateful.

"What does *that* mean?"

"Never mind." Leaning back a little, she gave him a gentle poke in the side. "Turn around and let's get going before Señor *Federal* decides to come after us. We're going to have to disguise you and find a change of clothes."

"Disguise me?" Owen nudged Sunflower in the ribs with his heels. "How?"

"You'll see. Just find a general store."

Owen cast a look over his shoulder and found Benny's eyes twinkling. "I have a feeling I'm not going to like whatever you're cooking up."

"You want to stay with me, you're going to have to do this my way."

Unable to get her to come clean, Owen had to content himself with the full-time task of keeping Sunflower's attention off the wild onions growing along the side of the road.

He could not wait to trade in this contrary, spavined animal for a vehicle with wheels. Cousin Jorge had better have a decent selection.

"I look like an Elvis impersonator!"

Benny surveyed Owen critically in the wavy, speckled mirror. She thought she'd done a pretty good job, considering she'd never been to cosmetology school and hadn't dyed her own hair since she was fourteen. Back then she'd gone in for magenta and green streaks or a full-platinum bleach. She wrinkled her nose. Thank goodness those days were over.

On the outskirts of Poza Rica, they'd stopped at the first general-store-cum-tourist-trap they came to. Leaving Owen to tend to the mule, Benny had gone inside to purchase a beach towel, a bottle of hair dye, a hat and a pair of cheap sunglasses.

She'd had to get creative to find a place to effect Owen's disguise. The restroom in the store was out of the question. Slipping a man of Owen's height past the clerk would have been impossible, and besides, anybody could walk in on them. So they'd headed toward town until they saw an outhouse in an empty schoolyard. It was relatively clean and contained a sink and mirror—the major requirements for Benny's impromptu beauty salon. Propping the door open, she'd draped the gaudy towel around Owen's broad shoulders and got to work.

Now his blond hair and eyebrows were jet black. By contrast, his horrified blue-green eyes looked even more electric. She had to admit, he bore a strong resemblance to the King, whose black-velvet portrait hung over the couch in Roxanne Gonzales's living room. Every day during her sophomore and junior years of high school, Benny had giggled at that portrait as she walked into the kitchen for breakfast.

She whipped the towel off his shoulders. "Can you do 'That's All Right, Mama'?"

Giving her a pained look, he slipped on a wrinkled

Hawaiian shirt he'd had stuffed in his backpack and buttoned it up. "You're making fun of me."

"Would I do that?" She crammed his discarded T-shirt and the towel into the backpack. Fooling around with Owen's hair had been an intimacy that left her flustered.

"What are you gonna do with *your* hair?"

"What do you mean?"

"You ought to cut it."

"Oh, no you don't!" She grabbed the braid lying across her shoulder. "If I cut this off I'll look like a Brillo pad." Vehemently she plopped on her new straw sun hat. "The hit man saw me wearing a skirt, with my hair down. See? In these jeans, with my head covered, I'll look like a boy."

There was a short silence as Owen studied her. "I don't think so." The look in his eyes seemed to suck every bit of oxygen out of the room.

Or maybe she was just breathless because it smelled so bad in here. "You s-said you wouldn't—"

Owen sighed. "I know, but…"

There was nothing threatening in his stance, and his gaze was tender. Still, she closed her eyes. Was she afraid of him or herself? She couldn't help thinking of that picture of her in his notebook.

"Bernadette, look at me."

She was trying to summon the courage to open her eyes when someone banged on the door. With extreme vigor. Apparently it had swung shut while she was occupied with Owen's hair.

"What's going on in there?" demanded a female voice in scandalized Spanish. "Get out here right now or I'll call the police!"

FIVE

Owen stared down into Benny's wide brown eyes. He'd been *this* close to kissing her. What kind of jerk kissed a woman for the first time in an outhouse?

The pounding on the door got louder. "Open up! What's going on in there?"

He shook his head to regain his composure. "I'll handle it." Yanking open the door, he found a middle-aged woman who, from every indication, was an out-of-work schoolteacher. "*¡Hola,* señora!" he said in the worst Texas accent he could muster. "*Gracias por* letting us *usar el baño. Yo estoy embarasado*—" He stopped when the woman's eyes widened and Benny gasped. "What? What did I say?"

"You know you just told her you were pregnant, you dork!" She looked as if she didn't know whether to laugh or faint.

"Oops." Pleased that his diversion had worked, he turned back to the woman still blocking the doorway. Her florid face was convulsing in laughter. "*Lo siento,* señora. *Yo no embarasado.* Yo— Yo—"

"Yo-yo about covers it." Benny ducked under his

arm to smile up at the señora. "We are sorry if we weren't supposed to be here," she said in her flawless Spanish. She had an ear for colloquialisms and she'd already picked up the penchant for extra x's and z's characteristic of the dialect in this part of Mexico. "We're having a very bad hair day."

Owen clutched his dyed locks. *That* was the under-statement of the year.

"We were just leaving," Benny continued. "Do you know where we can find the car lot of Jorge de Oca?"

The woman wiped her streaming eyes. "The other side of town on Highway 130 near the Poza Rica Inn. Jorge has fine cars, but I hope you have plenty of money. He does not sell cheap." She moved aside, glancing at Owen with mild disapproval. "You should let your wife do the talking if you expect to make a bargain."

"I'm not his—"

Owen bent down to lay a quick kiss on Benny's mouth. "*Sí,* señora," he said with a wink at the school-teacher. "*Hasta luego.*" He hustled Benny toward the gate, where they'd left Sunflower. "Ha. That went pretty well." He untied the mule and mounted, then reached a hand down for Benny.

"Depends on your definition of *well.*" She grabbed his wrist and let him boost her up. "If you wanted to make sure she remembers us, I'd say you accomplished your mission." She sighed as Owen nudged the mule's ribs. Sunflower brayed and reluctantly abandoned the weeds along the fence. "Doesn't Border Patrol ever do undercover work?"

"Benny, I'm a pilot. I generally wear a uniform." He patted her hand, lightly splayed across his middle. "This is a big city. The chances of anybody finding us here are next to nil."

"It's that little possibility that worries me."

Silence fell as Sunflower plodded along the street. It had been recently paved and the smell of sticky tar rose from the sunbaked road. Owen longed for a cold shower. Well, truthfully, he needed a cold shower for a lot of reasons. He and Benny were going to be together for a while, whether she liked it or not.

The problem would disappear if they were to get married. A thought that proved the sun had roasted his brain, too. He might be halfway in love with Benny, but he wasn't ready to marry a woman who had people shooting at her.

Yesterday. Had it been less than thirty-six hours ago that they'd taken off from the beach with bullets flying after them?

Owen pulled the mule to a halt in the shadow of a little adobe church whose steep roof was topped by a small bell tower. The bells began to chime for afternoon mass. "Bernadette, we've got to talk about this. Who's after you?"

She sat silent for a moment. "There are several possibilities."

The mule sidled. Owen settled him, tamping down irritation. "I can't help you if you won't give me a clue who they are."

He felt a gusty sigh against his back. "I know. I just… Owen, I'm not putting my life in somebody else's hands again—" She paused. "Nobody's but the Lord's."

"Yeah, that sounds really noble and spiritual, except for the fact that it's downright unbiblical." He felt her stiffen. Right about now his big brother would have told him to keep his mouth shut and wait for a better time to talk. But Owen had never been a big fan of waiting. Or keeping his mouth shut, for that matter. "What about the whole 'two are better than one' thing? And 'pity the man who falls and has no one to help him up'?" He prepared to defend himself. After all, who was he to correct somebody with a seminary Ph.D.?

"Okay, I give. You're right."

"I'm—what?" He looked over his shoulder and found her eyes closed, brows pulled together.

"I had no idea you knew so much Scripture. But you're right. It's not fair to expect you to hang with me and not tell you what's going on."

"So—" he struggled to regain his footing "—so you're going to fill me in?"

"No. We're splitting up as soon as we get to the car lot."

"Benny, we are not going through that rigmarole again. If you try to leave me, I'll find you. And you should know, I've got a wall full of tracking awards. Besides, you have no money and no ID. How do you think you'd get to Texas by yourself?"

"I can walk and I can hitchhike."

"You can hitchhike." He felt like howling.

"I don't want to, but I can. Owen, please." Her voice wobbled a little, the first crack in her pigheaded confidence he'd heard. "Please don't push me. There are things I can't say without putting other people in danger. I—I really feel safer when you're with me but not if you're going to keep on at me."

With a frustrated grunt, he kicked the mule into motion again and they continued to plod down the road.

That little waver in her voice got to him, whether he liked it or not.

His thoughts rotated like a propeller. What could Benny have done to make someone want to kill her? What was so bad, so scary that she refused to let him get involved?

As they rounded a bend in the road, a huge white sign painted with red letters appeared: Carros de Segunda Mano de Jorge. Jorge's Secondhand Cars.

They had other things to think about now, but he wasn't giving up on digging the information out of her. Nope, he didn't like to wait, but he could do it when he had to.

"I still think we should take a bus." Benny tugged on Sunflower's reins. Multicolored plastic flags flapped overhead as she peered through a chain-link fence at rows and rows of cars. Just inside the gate squatted the small prefab office building.

She and Owen had walked the last couple of blocks, leading the mule. Riding double through town, they had attracted a good bit of attention. Even with his hair dyed black and the sunglasses covering those brilliant eyes, Owen's height and military bearing made him stand out in a culture of small, wiry people who generally took life casually.

"I'm not riding public transportation unless we have to."

Benny looked up to find Owen's mouth set in a stubborn line. He and Sunflower had a lot in common.

"Why spend our little bit of money on a car? How are we going to buy gas? Come on, what's the matter? Has the daring ace pilot got a bus phobia?"

"Not exactly." He folded his arms. "Let's just say I'm

not in the mood to share a ride with a flock of chickens."

Sunflower, patently bored with the discussion, wheezed and lipped the daisies on Benny's hat. Laughing, she pushed his whiskery muzzle away. "Dinner at eight, big guy."

"Come on." He opened the gate and held it for Benny to lead the mule through. "Let's just talk to Cousin Jorge and see what kind of deal he'll offer."

Arguing with Owen was about as productive as blowing bubbles in a tornado. She followed him to the office. "All right, I'll let you do the talking. But no more *embarasado* stuff."

"You're such a killjoy." He grinned at her and knocked on the office door.

"*¡Hola, amigos!*" called a friendly male voice. "*Estaré pronto.*" A broad little man in neat, dark slacks and a white dress shirt appeared in the open doorway. With a beaming smile and three chins, he looked both prosperous and cordial. "*¡Americanos!*" He offered Owen a hand to shake. "*Me llama* Jorge de Oca. *¿En qué puedo ayúdarles hoy?*" What can I do for you today?

"We bring greetings from your cousin Gustavo," Owen said in Spanish. "He sent us to you for a reliable vehicle."

"Gustavo sent you?" Eyes popping, Jorge stood on tiptoe to peer over Owen's shoulder. "That's Sunflower! He never lets that mule out of his sight."

"We've been treating Sunflower like one of our own children." Owen patted the mule's neck. "Gustavo said you'd take care of him until he can come get him in a few days."

Jorge's smile dimmed. "I have no place to keep a mule."

"But Gustavo said—"

"Can I help it if my cousin won't move into the twenty-first century? He can't understand that the world is no longer one big goat farm."

"Listen, we'll pay you to feed the mule. Just tie him to the fence behind your building. Gustavo will come get him in a couple of days. We *have* to have a car."

The car dealer heaved a grand sigh, then stuck his head inside the office. "Carlota, I will be right back. I have customers." He waddled past Owen toward the mule. "I am interested in what brings two rich Americans to a used-car lot on a mule."

"Not all Americans are rich." Benny pulled Sunflower back. "We're missionaries headed back to the United States."

"I see." Jorge's black eyes gleamed. "Then how did you come upon my cousin's animal? Perhaps you're lying. Maybe you robbed poor Gustavo. I think I should call the police."

Benny gasped. "Please, no, we're—"

"I thought you were going to let *me* do the talking." Owen stepped between Jorge and Benny. "Come on, man, give us a break."

"I will give you a break." Jorge burst out laughing. "I should be on TV! I had you going, didn't I! Ah, you should see your faces! Tell me what you're looking for." Jorge tied the mule with a neat knot to the fence. "Car? Truck? SUV?"

"Truck," said Owen as Benny simultaneously said, "Car."

They looked at one another.

"Car," said Owen reluctantly and Benny smiled. He was such a guy.

"All right. Two-door or sedan?" Jorge led the way toward the first row of cars. Benny was pleasantly surprised to see that most of them appeared in fine condition.

"Doesn't matter," Owen said. "Just needs to be reliable and…uh…cheap."

Jorge halted. "Cheap? How cheap?"

"Well, I have three hundred American dollars," said Owen.

Jorge's genial expression evaporated into suspicion. "I do not have anything on my lot for three hundred dollars. Gustavo knows this. Are you sure he sent you?"

"Of course he sent us. Just ask Sunflower." Owen pulled out his wallet. "Look, can't we work out some kind of financing? Maybe use a credit card?"

"I am sorry, but I run a cash-only enterprise." Jorge stuck his hands into the pockets of his trousers and rocked on his heels like a Weeble.

Benny unobtrusively tugged on Owen's shirtsleeve. "Forget it," she said in English. "We can just take the bus."

"I'm not taking the bus!" Looking harassed, he turned back to the car dealer. "Jorge, let's talk." He threw an arm around the shorter man's shoulders. They walked off together, leaving Benny muttering her frustration to the mule.

"Men!" She jerked at the brim of her hat, which, along with a pair of red sunglasses, hid the top part of her face and provided shade against the relentless sun. "He doesn't get how much danger we're in."

But maybe Owen refused to take the situation seriously because she'd kept him in the dark. Was she being prudent or just selfish and paranoid? If Grenville found out Owen had been with her for the past two days, he'd assume she'd told him everything anyway. Owen's life—and maybe his career—were probably already compromised.

Oh, Lord, she prayed silently out of habit, *please give me more wisdom. Help me know how much to trust Owen, and please help him get hold of a car for us. Not just any old car—we need the* right *car. Preferably one that's full of gas.*

She opened her eyes and smiled to find the mule munching her daisies again. "And thank You for Sunflower," she said aloud, patting the animal's bony shoulder.

A few minutes later the men returned. Jorge laughed as Owen whacked him on the back.

Owen's white teeth were gleaming in his sun-bronzed face. "We've got a classic ride. You're gonna love it."

"More classic than Sunflower?" Benny had a bad feeling about this.

"Just wait 'til you see. Come on." Owen reached out a hand and Benny was so abstracted she took it without protest, letting him tug her toward the rear of the lot. He grinned over his shoulder. "I know you're attached to that mule, but you've got to leave him with Cousin Jorge."

"Oh. Okay." She tossed the reins to the car dealer, who smiled in what Benny considered entirely too enthusiastic a manner. "*Vaya con Dios,* Sunflower. *Gracias,* Jorge."

Jorge chuckled and waved before turning back to his office. The last Benny saw of him as she and Owen turned down a second lane of cars was Jorge swatting the mule's hindquarters with his hat.

"Will Sunflower be okay here?" Owen seemed to be in an awful hurry. "Maybe we should call Gustavo to let him know we got here safely."

"They don't have a phone." Owen walked faster. "Sunflower will be fine." He stopped at the end of the row of cars. "Madam, your chariot awaits."

All she saw were trucks. "I thought you agreed to get a car."

"This *is* a car. Meet Chitty Chitty Bang Bang." He dropped her hand.

She followed him to the other side of a maroon king-cab pickup. Squatting there like a powder-blue go-cart was a little Dodge with an unmistakably '60s-era body. Its left rear bumper had apparently had a close encounter with a light pole.

She swallowed. "Owen…"

"It's got push-button gears, can you believe that?" Owen slid into the driver's seat. "Come here."

Benny leaned in the open window. "This was all you could get for three hundred dollars?"

Owen pressed his lips together. "Yep."

"Owen, this thing's got to be close to fifty years old!"

"I *told* you—it's a classic! No telling how much I'll be able to get for it back in the States. Jorge didn't even know what he had." He slid his glasses to the top of his head and smiled up at her. "Come on, get in and let's see what she'll do."

"You mean you didn't drive it? What if it doesn't run?"

"Then I'll get my…my money back."

Benny frowned. There was something he wasn't telling her.

"Don't worry, I'm a great mechanic. Come on, Benny."

How could she resist that wheedling tone? Or the dimples?

Resigned, she released a breath. "Well, if this is all we could afford, it's all we could afford." She walked around to the passenger side, brushing her hand across the crushed fender.

Lord, is this Your idea of the perfect car?

In the course of this long and frustrating day, Briggs had discovered that Mexico was a highly inconvenient place to lose a target. Chartering an afternoon flight from Nuevo Laredo this late in the day turned out to be a pain. The only element working in his favor was the celebrated Mexican penchant for graft. Good thing money was no object with the judge. This was getting to be an expensive chase.

It cost him five hundred bucks just to convince some taco pilot to shuttle him across the mountains of central Mexico into the dumpy little oil city of Poza Rica. At just after 4:00 p.m., he was lugging his travel bag across the tarmac at the Tajin airport.

No telling how far away the cop and the girl had gotten by now. They could be anywhere, and he still had a long drive out to the boonies with no visible transportation. Best to start in the last place they'd been seen.

He supposed he should be grateful for his small lead.

"*¡Buenas tardes,* señor!" A smiling female attendant held the door open as he entered the terminal. "*¡Bienvenida a* Poza Rica!"

Briggs responded with an inarticulate growl. His Spanish stunk, which made this enterprise doubly difficult.

Breathe, Ray, he told himself. *Think about the resort you'll be sitting in when this is over.* "Taxi?"

Fortunately, that seemed to be one of those all-purpose international words. The woman nodded. "*Sí, taxi.*" She picked up the radio hooked to her belt and jabbered into it. "*Espera afuera.*" Her hand went out.

Everybody he bumped into wanted a tip. Grumbling, he opened his wallet and found a couple of pesos. She was just going to have to be happy with what he had.

It didn't take him long to navigate the little airport and find the taxi, which proved to be an ancient two-tone sedan with no rear bumper. The moment he got in, he started to wheeze. *Oh, brother.* He was going to be a dead man if he didn't get out of this filthy vehicle soon.

Nerves jangling, he twisted the cap off a twenty-ounce Mountain Dew he'd bought in Laredo. Maybe he should call the judge to say he was giving up.

Yeah, and end up like Frank Carter.

Last year, two weeks after failing to make good on a search warrant, Carter arrived on his wife's doorstep packed in three separate suitcases. Nobody knew for sure whether the judge had anything to do with that, but Ray wasn't one to take chances.

Besides, he was good at his job, and the pay was outstanding. He was going to retire young and live in one of those Mexican resorts like Cancún. Or maybe he'd have fun in Acapulco. *Yeah, me and Elvis.*

His shoulders tensed. Carmichael was Border Patrol, a close-knit and protective brotherhood. Surely the agency was aware of his disappearance by now. Wouldn't somebody go looking for him? If he didn't hurry, he was going to find himself outfoxed.

Okay, Ray, think. They would have to have transportation north. Bus? Car? Train even? No way of knowing.

He leaned his head back, sweating in misery. If only he'd hit the girl when he'd had her in his sights. But he hadn't, so he'd just have to deal with it. If you had money and persistence, information could be bought. Surely somebody would have noticed a big blond border cop and a Polynesian-looking beauty queen on the road.

Draining the bottle of Mountain Dew, he tried harder to breathe.

Briggs, you've got a job to do.

SIX

"Who are you calling?"

"Eli." Owen glanced at Bernadette as he plugged a couple of coins into the phone. The lobby of the Poza Rica Inn, where they'd stopped for a meal in the hotel restaurant and a bathroom break, was nothing to write home about. But at least it was clean.

He and Benny both looked like they'd been "rode hard and put up wet," as his dad used to say. She would never be less than beautiful, but there were shadows painted under her exotic brown eyes, and she kept nibbling her thumbnail. He knew she was anxious to get on the road again.

"Somebody in the States needs to know where we are. They'll be worried about us."

"I guess you're right." Bernadette rubbed her arms, though a lethargic overhead fan barely stirred the air. "I used to get really mad at Meg when she left her cell uncharged for days on end. But don't tell Eli too much or he and Isabel will just worry more."

"How much is too—" He stopped when the dial tone was interrupted by an operator who told him how much money to put into the phone. He chunked in more coins as Bernadette paced to the poolside door for the third time. She was making him dizzy. He'd never seen her so keyed up. At last he got a ring tone.

Come on, Eli. Answer your cell phone.

"Carmichael here."

"Eli, it's Owen."

"Hey! Where are you?" Eli's usually measured voice was clipped, tense. "We expected you back yesterday. Called the airport and they said you never filed a flight plan. Mom's about to go crazy!"

"I'm at a hotel in Poza Rica. With Bernadette. Listen, we're in trouble—"

"What kind of trouble? Owen, so help me if you ever pull something like this again—"

"Eli, shut up and listen. I was getting ready to leave yesterday morning, but some thug came after Benny with a submachine gun, so I had to take her up without filing a—"

"After her with *what?* Owen, if this is one of your stupid jokes—"

"It's no joke." Benny stood looking out at the pool, both hands spread on the glass. Beyond her the sun glared off water so blue it hurt his eyes. He wished he could do something to comfort her.

He could almost hear Eli trying to absorb what Owen himself could barely comprehend—even though he'd been right there, seen it with his own eyes.

"What's going on down there?" Eli finally said.

"Okay, quick version—we need to get out of here. The shooter put holes in both gas tanks, so I had to make an emergency landing in a cow pasture.

Cracked a wing on a tree. We borrowed the farmer's mule to make the trip here to Poza Rica, which took most of the day. We just bought a car and we're headed north."

"What can I do to help?"

He turned away and lowered his voice. "Eli, there's something weird going on with Benny. She won't tell me who's after her or why. Says it'll get somebody else in trouble. I'm going along with it for now, because I—" He stopped. Why *was* he going along with it? Because he didn't want to know what she'd done to get somebody mad enough to kill her?

"Because what?"

Owen took a breath. "Because I don't want her running into something she can't handle. We're down here with very little money. Benny's got no ID, and for some reason she's in a big hurry to get to Memphis. Here's what I want you to do. Call Meg Torres and see what you can find out. She knows Bernadette's background."

"Meg and Jack are in D.C. now. You sure you want to involve them?"

"Why not? Jack's with Homeland Security, and he's got connections out the wazoo."

"How am I going to get hold of you? Where's your phone?"

"I've got it, but the battery's almost dead. I'm saving it for emergencies. Besides, cell reception down here's unpredictable. I'll call you when I get to another pay phone. In the meantime, just find out what you can."

"I will. Listen—" Eli paused "—I really think I need to come down there and get you guys."

Owen hesitated. He depended on his brother a lot, but they weren't that desperate yet. "No, I can handle it."

"All right, then. I'm praying for you, brother."

"Thanks. We need it."

Owen hung up and walked up behind Bernadette. She'd taken off her hat and held it by the strings, so all he could see was curly hair spiraling halfway down her back. "Eli knows what's going on. You ready to go?"

She turned, her back against the door. "I doubt there's anything Eli can do about it." Her voice was as stiff as her shoulders.

He hated feeling helpless. "Bernadette, we'll get home. We'll figure this out. I won't let anybody hurt you."

"You're not God. That's not always for you to say." She pressed her fingers into her eyes. He wanted to put his arms around her, so he tucked his hands under his armpits. "I made choices a long time ago that set this whole thing in motion. And God's allowing it. I don't know why, but He is."

"So this is a martyr thing?" Owen stepped back, hands raised. "You just give up and say 'Come and get me'?"

"Of course not." Bernadette looked away. "I'm just saying you can't protect me from the consequences of my own actions."

"I'm thinking that the woman you are now is a whole lot more important than whatever you did in the past." He reached out and brushed his thumb across a damp spot on her cheek. "Bernadette, let me...let me..." He didn't even know what he wanted. There was no way to finish that sentence. He stuffed his hands into his pockets. "Come on, let's check out the restaurant. Might as well get a decent meal while we have the chance."

* * *

By the time the taxi pulled up to the Poza Rica Inn, Briggs was steaming. No amount of gesturing, shouting or pointing to the map had served to get the driver to go where he actually wanted to end up. Apparently, every American went straight from airport to hotel without stopping to pass Go or collect two hundred dollars.

Infuriating.

So, after some arguing over the fare—a pointless exercise since he had no idea what the guy was saying— he got out and tossed some pesos through the window. Maybe somebody in the hotel could speak English.

He'd have sold his soul for a shot of whiskey, but that wasn't gonna happen. *Get this over with. Track them down and move on.*

Inside the lobby, a teenage girl dressed in an I Love New York T-shirt sat at the desk. Flipping through a magazine, she bobbed her head in rhythm with whatever was coming through her headphones. He walked up to her and whacked his hand on the desk.

"*¡Señorita!*"

The girl looked up and yanked off the headphones. "*¿Sí?*"

"Do you speak English?"

"*Sí.* I mean, yes. You like to hook up, señor?"

"Hook up?" What was this, a brothel? "No, I just want directions."

The girl's face fell. "Directions to where?"

"Here." He pulled out his map of Veracruz and stubbed his finger on the area just southeast of Poza Rica. "And I need transportation."

"Transportation?" She looked confused.

"Car," he enunciated carefully. "Bus. Something with wheels. I have to find this farm."

"You need a taxi?" She picked up the phone.

"No! I just got out of a taxi." He pulled out his wallet and removed a twenty-dollar bill. "Where can I rent a car?"

The girl brightened. "My uncle Jorge has cars on the next street over." She glanced at the twenty. "I could call him for you."

"No, thank you, I'll walk. Which direction?"

"I draw a map." She rooted in a drawer and extracted a paper napkin and a pen.

"All right. And while you're at it, write down the quickest way to get to that area of the map."

While he waited, Ray glanced across the lobby. A tall, dark-haired man wearing a goofy tourist shirt, accompanied by a young boy in a straw hat, had just disappeared into the restaurant. Maybe they were Americans and spoke English. He was just about to go after them and find out when the desk clerk finished her drawing.

"Here, señor." She pushed the scrap of paper toward him. "Tell my uncle that Alita sent you."

Ray hadn't eaten since early that morning and he was starved. But the sooner he got this business over with, the better.

"Thanks, *querida*." He slid her the twenty. "I don't suppose your uncle speaks English, does he?"

Benny took a bite of her cheese-and-tomato sandwich. Owen had already finished his grilled chicken and black beans and was looking at the dessert menu.

He had been very quiet since leaving the hotel lobby, and she hadn't had much to say, either.

The look in his eyes when he'd brushed his thumb across her cheek… Okay, she'd seen it before. Or something similar. There was the young doctor in Fort Worth, a friend of her roommate, Meg. She and Elliot had been bowling together a few times. But when he tried to get her to give up on going to Mexico, she'd finally realized he was way more serious than he needed to be. So she'd had to give him a less-than-gentle heave-ho.

And there was a single pastor in Acuña, a widower with a bevy of children aged six all the way up to sixteen. He'd seemed interested in more than shoptalk when they ran into each other.

But she didn't want to get married to a man she didn't love just for his convenience.

She watched Owen for a moment, hoping he wouldn't catch her at it. He whistled through his teeth, eyeing the pictures of the desserts with obvious enjoyment. She would never have imagined dark hair would suit him, but it did. He could even carry off a shirt with lime-green parakeets all over it.

What was she going to do about him?

Bernadette, let me…

Let him *what?* What did he want? He could have any woman he wanted back in Del Rio. She'd watched them go after him with single-minded determination, and he never seemed to notice. Isabel said he'd occasionally take a woman out, then never call her again. Why? Was he just that flighty?

People said he was a player, shallow as a roadside ditch, but she didn't believe it. She'd seen depths in him over the past two days that put him on her short list of dependable people.

Which was why it shook her to the core, this realization that his emotions might be genuinely engaged where she was concerned. She dreaded hurting him.

He put down the menu and smiled. "Want to share some fried ice cream?"

She pushed away her discomfort. "Why not? Better eat while we can. We've got a long drive ahead of us tonight."

"Are you sure you still want to do that? I could get us a couple of rooms, put it on my credit card—"

"No! You know how that would look. We've got to keep going."

He sighed. "All right. I just thought I'd give it one more shot. Under the circumstances, nobody's going to give our being together a second thought."

In her experience, most people would think the worst. But she wasn't going to argue with him. She picked up the menu. "Make sure you ask for two spoons. Fried ice cream's my favorite thing in the world."

Hands above his shoulders, Briggs stared into the barrel of the scruffy little farmer's shotgun. He had no idea how to say "Don't shoot" in Spanish.

Wasn't this just par for the course? First, that oily car dealer in Poza Rica had gouged him for at least twice the worth of a gas-guzzling Crown Victoria—after insisting it was the only vehicle available for lease. Then he missed a turn off the highway because major landmarks had been either moved or destroyed completely.

Once he realized his mistake, he'd stopped a group of bicyclers headed for the beaches. Using his well-thumbed Spanish phrase book, he'd haltingly asked for directions. With much gesturing and laughter—apparently the American plane's impromptu landing strip had become quite the community conversation piece—the three youths steered him back in the direction he'd come from. An hour later, he found himself meandering twelve miles down a bumpy one-lane track until he reached the dilapidated farm of Gustavo de Oca.

And it had gone downhill from there.

When he drove into the barnyard, the Cessna was in plain sight, wedged nose first into the side of a barn. But nary a soul appeared to greet him. Road-weary, hungry and suffering from allergies that threatened to turn into a migraine, he'd stomped toward the plane.

He had his cell phone out, trying to get hold of the judge, when he'd felt the gun jam into his lower back.

"*Buenos dias,* señor." Unable to reach the phrase book in his back pocket, he'd slowly turned. "*¿Amigo?*" Why had he left his own gun in the trunk of the car? He had a permit to carry it.

The farmer's fierce mustache turned down a notch. "*¿Qué hace usted con mi avión?*"

He might as well have been speaking Chinese. "Sorry. *No comprende.*" Ray wiggled his fingers. "Just looking for some people. *Hombres.*" Keeping eye contact, he cautiously lowered one hand and tugged the phrase book out of his pocket. "*Un momento.*"

The gun was still shoved into his abdomen, but at least it didn't go off. Farmer de Oca watched suspiciously as he flipped through the booklet.

"Busco por piloto." Ray *hoped* he'd just said he was looking for the pilot.

The farmer shook his head. *"No está."*

"Well, obviously he's not—" Breaking off in frustration, he searched the book again. *"Dónde—"* He turned a few more pages. *"¿Dónde ellos ir?"*

"Poza Rica."

Ray's mouth fell open. He'd just come from Poza Rica. "How did they get there? Did they say where they were headed?"

De Oca's heavy brows twitched together. He shrugged. *"No hablo inglés."*

Muttering, Ray looked it up. *"¿Como?"* How?

The farmer burst into guffaws. *"En mi burro."* He pantomimed riding a horse. Mercifully, he lowered the gun first.

So they took off on a horse to Poza Rica. That still gave him no idea where to start looking.

"Gracias, señor." He backed toward the Crown Victoria, keeping an eye on the shotgun. "I leave now. *Adiós."*

The farmer was still grinning. *"Apuesto que Jorge estaba soprendido."*

Ray halted. "Jorge? Jorge de Oca?"

"Sí, sí." De Oca wagged his shaggy head. *"Mi primo. Les dije que le compraran un carro de él."*

Ray understood the word *car,* and looked up *primo.* Cousin. He groaned. He should have known the family name wasn't any coincidence. He had wasted nearly three hours on a wild-goose chase when his targets had been right under his nose.

If that didn't just beat all.

* * *

Owen loved engines almost as much as he loved horses. The little blue car hit a sweet spot that nearly overcame his guilt at having abandoned Sunflower to the less-than-tender mercies of Cousin Jorge. Knowing how much money he was going to make when he auctioned it on eBay also eased his regret when he looked at the blank spot on his right hand.

Benny sat with her back against the passenger door, her long, curly hair blowing in the warm breeze coming through the open windows. Now *that* was a sight calculated to lift a man's spirits. Maybe they were running for their lives or running to some unknown rendezvous— frankly, he *still* didn't know exactly what was going on— but it was springtime on the coast of Mexico and he was driving a classic car with a beautiful woman by his side.

It's all good, Lord.

But come to think of it, she'd been awfully quiet for the last couple of hours. Mostly she watched the mountains pass to their left, but every once in a while, she turned to look at him in a thoughtful way that made his skin prickle.

"What are you thinking about?"

"I was just wondering what made you decide to be a pilot."

He relaxed and smiled. "Shingles."

She blinked and laughed. "Shingles? You mean, like the disease?"

"No." He chuckled. "Like on the roof. One summer when I was really little, maybe three or four, my mom went out of town for the weekend and left Dad in charge." He grinned, remembering. "He was roofing the house and Eli must've been old enough to help.

They nailed my pants to the roof with a tenpenny nail to keep me from falling off. I lay there on my back for hours, watching the planes fly over."

Her eyes widened. "Sounds like child abuse." Then she smiled. "I bet you were a busy little guy."

"That's an understatement. I never walked anywhere if I could run and never used my feet if I could ride. Horses, tractors, four-wheelers—whatever. I must've jumped off the roof of the barn five times before my mother wore out my behind enough times to convince me that wasn't a good idea."

She winced. "Broken bones?"

"Collarbone, left arm—which was a disaster, since I'm left-handed—and—" he tapped his cheekbone "—see this scar? I fell on a pitchfork one time." He shook his head. "I could've killed myself, I guess, but somebody was watching out for me."

"Apparently so. What did your parents think when you got your pilot's license?"

"They didn't know for a long time." He shrugged. "You know how, when you're a kid, you can rationalize all kinds of deception? Didn't want to worry them, so I told just enough of the truth to keep them in the dark. When they found out I'd been working as a grunt at the airport—we were living in Laredo at the time— to comp flying lessons, I was grounded for six months. Eventually, though, they realized I was serious about it and gave me their blessing."

She was quiet for a minute, staring out the windshield, and Owen let the miles roll past. How long would it take her to feel comfortable telling him about what had turned her into such a closed book?

Weird way to think of a woman who daily put herself on the line for other people. He'd seen her tenderness with children, the elderly, sick or wounded…emotionally scarred women. But he'd never seen her open her own personal box of limitations, and she generally walked a wide circle around men.

He was no psychologist, but that had to be a big glaring clue. Some man had left a scar on her that she'd never gotten over. Did the man they were running from now have something to do with it?

He glanced at her again. Her expression was pensive, her elegant hands folded in her lap. She could be so still. He supposed if he had an IQ like hers, he could entertain himself with his own thoughts, too.

"When did you decide you wanted to become a missionary?"

She jumped a little, as though she'd been miles away. "It wasn't a conscious decision. While I was living in Mississippi, the Gonzaleses were always going somewhere or other on mission trips. They finally talked me into going with them to help paint a dormitory for a homeless ministry in Fort Worth. That's where I accepted Christ as my Savior."

"No kiddin'." Now they were getting somewhere. Maybe she just had to be really, really tired before she opened up. They'd certainly had a long day.

"Yeah." She sighed. "Seeing other people worse off than me—who could sing and praise God anyway—changed me in a way I can't even describe. I fell in love with Jesus and couldn't get enough of Him. I memorized—" She stopped, looking self-conscious. "I found I had an aptitude for learning Scripture quickly."

Slowing to negotiate a pothole, Owen waited for Benny to finish her thought. She didn't. "How much?"

"Hmm?"

"How much Scripture have you memorized, Bernadette?"

She shrugged, blushing. "I know most of the book of John and Paul's letters. Big hunks of Genesis and the Psalms. All of the books of Esther and Ruth." When he goggled at her, she wrinkled her nose. "It's just a gift I have, like yours with flying."

"That's not a gift—it's an affliction."

Her husky giggle filled him with something so sweet it was almost tangible, like ice cream sliding over his tongue. He savored it for a minute until it scared him because he wanted to stop the car and kiss her.

And he knew how well *that* would go over. He cleared his throat. "So why Mexico? You could've stayed in the U.S. to work in an orphanage."

"I know. And I almost did. In fact, while I was in seminary, I worked in a halfway house run by the Texas Youth Commission."

"You worked with juvie criminals?"

"For about three years. But it was so frustrating when we'd lose one back to the streets. After all, I'd been—I mean, I could imagine what they were going through."

Owen hadn't missed her halt and redirect. Instincts on alert, he was more determined than ever to dig the past out of her. Where *had* she been? What had happened that she could so strongly identify with a bunch of teenage delinquents?

"Anyway," she continued, "by the time I got out of seminary, there was a huge need for bilingual house-mothers to work with the Texas River Ministry. I know you understand the problem with teenage prostitution in the border cities." She glanced at him and he nodded. "Kids have kids and they get abandoned to the streets. I had the skills and a desire to do something about it, so…that's where I wound up."

"I guess you've been happy there, huh?"

"I can't imagine doing anything else."

Owen liked his job, too, but it wasn't a passion that would make him give up living in America to deal daily with faulty electricity, chancy sewage and bad water.

At least, to this point it hadn't been. The Lord seemed to be saying something that was either couched in terms Owen wasn't familiar with, or that he simply didn't want to hear.

Fortunately, he didn't have to explore the feeling right then. A green road sign loomed.

"Hey, San Rafael's coming up. What do you say we find someplace to eat supper and—"

"Owen, that's a little bitty village. We don't have any more cash, remember?"

"Actually," he said sheepishly, "we do. A little."

"What?" Benny sat up. "Owen, what have you done?" She gasped. "You traded your ring! I knew something looked funny." She was staring at his hands on the steering wheel.

He flexed his fingers. "Yeah, so what? It's just a ring. I'll get another one."

"That was a very expensive ring, wasn't it? And I could tell it meant a lot to you." She was frowning, big dark-chocolate eyes troubled.

Over his class ring. He felt his mouth curling. Pretty sweet.

The nakedness of his finger suddenly felt okay. "Look, we'll be in the States by tomorrow morning. I'll call Jorge, wire him some money and get him to mail me the ring. No big deal."

"Owen, all this isn't going to magically disappear when we get to the States. I have to get to Memphis somehow, without—without calling attention to myself."

"All right, just don't sweat the ring. It was mine to give up. It served its purpose and I'm okay with it. Now, what are you in the mood to eat?"

There was no way to argue with a man whose temperament ranged from sunny to partly cloudy, so she gave up.

"I'm thinking burritos," she said with a grin.

SEVEN

Briggs reversed directions and hit Poza Rica just as Jorge de Oca was locking the gate on his car lot.

"*Cerrado,*" said de Oca firmly, jingling an officious-looking wad of keys.

But when Ray showed him a hundred-dollar bill, the gate swung wide open. "I keep the car," he said in halting Spanish after looking it up in the book. "Another short trip."

"*Sí, no problema,*" said the chubby car dealer. He all but pushed Ray out the gate again. The home fires were evidently burning.

"Wait!" Ray desperately flipped through the phrase book, trying to piece together the words *I want to find my niece.* "*Yo perdido mi sobrina.*" He glared at Jorge, who looked ready to call the men in white coats. "*¿Usted ver ella hoy?*" He brought out the picture of Bernadette Malone.

The dealer's eyes widened as he grinned. "*Caramba, sí, una chica muy bonita.*" He glanced at Ray, looking skeptical. "*Su sobrina?*" Your niece?

Ray nodded. "*¿Dónde?*" Where?

De Oca shrugged and pointed. "Poza Rica Inn, *tal vez.*"

"You have got to be kidding." What was a hit man supposed to do when his mark kept sliding out of his grasp like a wet bar of soap? He consulted his book. "*¿Qué carro?*" He gestured driving, hands on imaginary steering wheel.

De Oca beamed. "*Un clásico.* '65 Dodge."

"What color?"

"*Azul.*"

Ray looked that up and sighed in relief. A classic blue Dodge shouldn't be too hard to find.

"This is such a cliché." Benny peered around Owen's broad shoulders into the black hole under the little car's hood. As if she had any idea what she was looking at. "I thought you were a good mechanic."

Five minutes ago, the front of the car had given a loud *clunk,* and black smoke had poured out of the hood like steam from the nose of a cartoon *toro.* Owen had barely managed to keep the car from jolting onto the steep shoulder of the road.

"I'm a *great* mechanic," he muttered. "When I have the right parts."

"You should have driven it before we took it off the lot."

"What good would that have done? We came nearly three hundred miles before it blew." He pulled out the dipstick and wiped it off on the bottom of his shirt. "We've lost so much oil it's a wonder this didn't happen way back down the road."

"Great." She folded her arms. "Now we have hardly any money and you don't even have your ring as a backup."

"I have my credit cards."

She looked around at the desolate surroundings. Mountains to the left, open fields to the right and a long stretch of moonlit highway ahead and behind. "Oh, yeah, just whip out that Visa right here."

He let down the hood and rested his hands on it. "When did you develop this sarcastic streak?"

"It just comes out when I'm tired and hungry and scared." He had to be tired, too. They'd been traveling for almost five hours, and he'd done most of the driving. The sun had set like a big red beach ball over the mountains, and a full moon had bounced up to take its place. "I'm sorry, Owen. I can't believe you've stuck with me this long."

He really was the most amazing man. He'd done the best he could under the circumstances. It had to be killing him not to know what was going on. Not that she knew much. Ladonna had given her just the bare facts.

Celine. Tamika. Daisy. All dead. And Grenville had to be behind it.

She shuddered.

"What's the matter? You cold?"

There *was* a nip in the air, now that he mentioned it. This climate could fry you to a crisp during the middle of the day, then send you looking for a sweater at night. Good thing Owen had brought his denim jacket and was willing to share. She'd had to roll up the sleeves three or four times, but at least it was warm.

"I'm okay. But if we're going to make it to Ciudad Victoria, we'd better start walking." She opened the car door and grabbed the backpack.

"Let me have that." He took it from her without giving her a chance to refuse. Southern men, especially those in law enforcement, treated women with a courtesy bordering on chauvinism. She hardly noticed it most of the time, but tonight her nerves were on edge.

"Owen, I'm not some dainty little flower who's going into a fainting spell if I have to carry a backpack."

"I know you're not." He set off, pocketing the car keys. "Come on. Traffic's been pretty light today, but maybe somebody'll pass by and take pity on us."

She trotted after him. "I mean it. You're just as tired as I am."

"Are you *trying* to pick a fight?" She couldn't see his expression, but his tone was amused.

"Of course not." She halted. "What was that?"

"Hmm?"

"That noise. I heard something grunt."

"They should put your ears in the national registry. I didn't hear anything."

"Stop, Owen." She grabbed his wrist. "It sounds like a— Whoa. That is the biggest pig I've ever seen in my life!"

About twenty yards away, an enormous sow sashayed toward them right down the middle of the highway. Moonlight bathed her hairy pink hide and gleamed off the wobbling teats. Her snuffling grunts got louder and more indignant the closer she got.

Benny stepped closer to Owen. She didn't like the intent look in the animal's small eyes. "What's she doing out here all by herself?"

"I assume there's a farm close by and she got loose. You want to look around and see? Maybe they'd put us up for the night like the de Ocas did."

"If we leave the road we'll just get lost."

"I'm a professional tracker. I'm not going to get lost."
He gave Benny's hand a tug. "But if you want to walk
all night, it's no skin off my nose. Come on, she won't
hurt us as long as we don't bother her."

But the pig veered off the road straight at them,
grumbling porcine imprecations with every step. Snout
to the ground, she circled Benny and Owen, tail whip-
ping back and forth like a windshield wiper. She was a
gargantuan specimen, nearly as broad as she was tall,
her back reaching almost to Owen's knees.

"What is she doing?" Benny dove under Owen's arm.

He pulled her close and she could feel his laughter
rumbling under his rib cage. "Checking us out. Eli and
I had a potbelly pig when I was a teenager. Raised her
for the 4-H club. She was psycho, but she won the blue
ribbon at the fair three years in a row."

The pig had snuffled a complete circle around them.
Apparently deciding they meant no harm, she waddled
off in the direction she'd come.

"I think I'm insulted." Benny giggled.

"Let's see where she goes. I'm thirsty."

"As long as she stays on the road. I'm not venturing
off into the cactus."

They set off again, following their fat tour guide.
Though Owen ambled along at a relaxed pace, Benny
had to take an occasional skipping step to keep up.

"I take it you never lived on a farm." Owen hadn't let
go of her hand, and Benny didn't have the energy to
protest. His clasp was firm and protective, almost im-
personal. Besides, it was dark and she didn't want to trip.

"Are you kidding? I spent most of my time on the

streets of Memphis." At his dead silence, she realized what she'd said. "I mean, you know, I'm a real city girl."

He still didn't answer. Something about the brace of muscle in his arm set her nerves jangling.

"Owen?"

"I'm just wondering because you said you grew up in Collierville."

"I did. Collierville is kind of a suburb of Memphis."

"Oh. Okay." After a minute, he sighed. "Just tell me when you get ready, Benny. Why don't you sing me the rice pudding song? I didn't catch all the words."

Benny swallowed an unexpected thickness in her throat. Owen could surprise her with that sensitive streak. "Okay, but I'm no diva." She cleared her throat. *"Arroz con leche, me quiero casar con un mexicano que sepa cantar."*

Owen chuckled. "'I want to marry a Mexican who can sing.' Classic top-forty lyrics. What's the second verse?"

"El hijo del rey me manda un papel, me manda decir que me case con el."

"Okay, 'The son of the king gave me a paper'? What's that mean?"

"It's a nursery song. I don't think it's supposed to make much sense. Something about the prince sending an order to marry him. Then the last part is *'Con éste sí, con éste no, con éste mero, me caso yo.'*"

"'With this one yes, with this one no, with the simple man I will wed.' Every girl's dream, huh?" She felt his focus on her. "Is that what you want, Benny? A simple man? Somebody you can lead around by the nose?"

"Me?" She laughed. "I don't want a man at all."

"Hey, you gotta admit, we come in handy occasionally. How would you have gotten out of that pickle on the beach without me?"

"You simple guys have your uses," she teased. "What I mean is, I don't need to get married to be…complete."

"Oh, come on. Every girl wants to get married. Didn't you play with dolls and junk like that?"

"I suppose. A long, long time ago." So long ago she could barely remember it. "My mom and I were in a women's shelter one time and somebody gave us a shoe box full of toys for Christmas. There was a little plastic baby doll with a lacy dress and a hole in its mouth for the bottle."

She hadn't thought about that doll in a long time. That had been a happy Christmas. Then they'd gone back to Mama's boyfriend.

Owen squeezed her hand. "Guess that's where you got your sympathy for orphans, huh?"

"Maybe. But I went to the orphanage for a lot of reasons. When I finished seminary, they tried to get me to stick around and teach Hebrew. I turned the job down because I was tired of the classroom."

"Don't you ever want your own family? Babies?"

"Owen…" She'd prayed through this with Meg, gotten it off her heart. Revisiting the subject with a six-foot-two cowboy border cop, even in the intimacy of the dark and the pale moonlight, made her squirm.

"Come on, it's just your buddy Owen. Humor me. It's a long way to Ciudad Victoria."

My buddy? Hardly. "Let's just say I have some scars I wouldn't inflict on a husband."

"What do you mean?"

Apparently, the sensitive streak was over. She should tell him just enough to scare him off. "Every man wants to be first. I can't give that."

He absorbed her words in silence, then let out a breath. "I don't know many women nowadays who can."

"Owen, before I came to know Christ, I was…promiscuous." There. She'd said it. The bald and ugly truth.

"So was Mary Magdalene and she got to start over. I may be one of those simple men, but even I know that."

Why was he not shocked? He should be running away, fast and furious. If he knew the whole truth, he would. "Oh, Owen, I know that, too. I've forgiven myself, really. It's just that the consequences never go away."

Although most people wouldn't get drilled by a hit man….

"Is that what this is all about? An old boyfriend is out to get you?"

At the growl in his voice, she winced. "Something like that." But she wasn't going to give it any more space in her thoughts. The rage would come in and take over like it had so many times before. "Hey, I think I hear a car coming."

"Great. Here's our chance. You ever hitchhike?"

"Not in a long time."

"Okay. Watch the master." He turned to walk backward, right thumb held high.

The car sped toward them, a station wagon with massive headlights and grill. The reverberations of four mondo speakers, blasting salsa rock through the open windows, made the car bounce as if it were on springs. It zoomed past at about eighty miles an hour without even slowing down.

"Hey!" Owen lowered his arm, indignation in every line of his body. "What're they in such a big hurry for?"

Benny chuckled. "The noise would've given me a headache anyway. Try the next one."

"There may not *be* a next one." Owen shifted the backpack. "But let's hope there is."

"At least the closer we get to Ciudad Victoria, the more traffic there'll be."

Fortunately, a few minutes later, Benny heard another vehicle approach from behind. "Owen! Get ready to try again!"

"Good night, you've got supersonic hearing." But he turned backward again, wildly jerking his thumb as a black pickup truck barreled past. At least it honked on the way by.

"Maybe there's something wrong with your technique."

"What do you mean? There's no *technique*. You just stick out your thumb and look hopeful."

"Really? Then how come nobody's stopped yet?"

"There've only been two chances. Give me a break!"

"You know what this reminds me of? That old Clark Gable and Claudette Colbert movie. You know, where he does the Bugs Bunny impression with the carrot?"

"You mean *It Happened One Night?*" Owen laughed. "I think it was the bunny doing a Gable impression, not the other way around."

"Whatever. Remember how they finally got a ride?"

"Yeah, she stuck out her leg and lifted her skirt. You gonna try it?"

"I would, but I'm in pants."

"Sure you would…" Owen teasingly bumped her

elbow with his. "Miss Modesty. Anyway, you'd cause a traffic jam. We wouldn't want that."

Benny felt herself blush. That was a sweet thing to say, in a wrong-side-out kind of way. "Look, Big Mama's trotting right along. You think she smells food?"

"Beats me." The pig disappeared around a hairpin bend in the road. "Let's catch up and see." He started to jog and Benny ran to keep up.

A minute later, they reached the turn. Benny jerked to a halt.

Owen laughed. "Veracruz KOA."

The pig was waddling up to a fruit truck parked just off the road. A canvas awning on poles stretched across its bed and extended to form an open-sided tent. Beneath it, a family sat on wooden folding stools around an oil lamp.

Charming scene. Benny would love to have had Owen's camera out right then.

"Fernanda!" A little girl in pigtails who looked to be around ten ran to throw her arms around the sow. "Where have you been, you bad girl!" She looked up with a frightened gasp when Owen tugged Benny into the light. "Mama! Strangers!"

Owen lifted a hand. "We won't hurt anybody. Our car broke down back there—" he gestured over his shoulder "—and we've been following your pig."

The eldest member of the group, a grande dame in traditional embroidered dress and head scarf, rose from her stool, hands extended. "Welcome, children." Her dark, wizened face creased in a smile. "Come and rest with us."

* * *

Briggs could be charming when he chose to be. After all, he had been raised in a family whose Southern roots went all the way back to Jeb Stuart. However, for the past forty-eight hours he had been operating on no sleep, very little food and a truckload of frustration.

When he walked in the front door of the Poza Rica Inn and saw the same gum-chewing little Mexican Gen-Xer who'd waited on him previously, he came unglued.

"Your uncle is a crook!"

She removed her headphones. "Señor?"

"I said—" He started to wheeze just as his phone rang. He unclipped it from his belt and looked at the caller ID. "Boss!" he gasped. "How are you?"

"What's the matter with you, Briggs?" The sonorous voice was irritated. "I've been trying to call you for an hour. Where have you been?"

Ray glanced at the desk clerk. She had put her headphones back on and gone back to her magazine. Still, he walked into a corner where he was less likely to be overheard. "Sorry, boss. Cell reception down here stinks. I've been trying to track down the girl."

"Well, if you'd answered your phone, I would have told you where she was. The border cop used his credit card at the Poza Rica Inn restaurant."

"What? When?" Ray's migraine had just come on full force.

"About five hours ago. Talk to the waitstaff and find out if they heard anything."

Five hours ago. He had been standing here in this lobby, and the restaurant was right over—

He wheeled. The tall man in the tourist shirt and the

little boy in the straw hat. Could they have been…
What if Carmichael had dyed his hair and the girl had
changed clothes?

"Okay, boss, I'm on it." He shut the phone.

Owen sat on the outer edge of the family circle,
taking shots with his digital camera of Bernadette playing a clapping game with young Reyna Fronteras.
Reyna's father, Noé, accompanied the song on a small
acoustic guitar, while her mother, Ana Maria, and little
brother Jefe sang along. Elderly Marta of the head scarf
dozed on her stool, chin against her chest. Fernanda the
pig lay like a side of pork under the tailgate of the truck.

He focused the lens on Marta and pushed the shutter
button. If she'd been awake, he would have asked permission first, since elderly Mexicans were often super-
stitious about being photographed. The nexus of the
family, she had entertained them all with a story about
her first trip across the border to pick fruit at the end of
World War II. Then she'd fallen asleep with the abrupt-
ness of the innocent.

Snapping another picture of Benny and the little girl,
he let out a jaw-cracking yawn. He was dead on his feet,
too. He didn't know how Bernadette had the energy to
socialize after the day they'd had. This whole bizarre
series of events was turning into a spaghetti Western adventure. He found himself listening for the eerie whis-
tling of a wooden flute and watching for Clint Eastwood
to come riding up on a paint pony.

He was thankful for the Fronteras family. They
were headed to the border with a truckload of
mangoes, papayas, oranges and bananas. Not only

were he and Benny saving the money they would have spent on two hotel rooms, but they avoided the awkwardness of spending a night alone together. Benny's concern about that made more sense to him, now that he knew more about her background. He hoped he'd managed to hide his shock.

Promiscuous. The distasteful word conjured up all kinds of undesirable mental pictures. How many boyfriends had she had? Three? Five? He winced as he scrolled through the pictures he'd just taken. *Ten?*

Impossible to bring his image of gentle, straight-arrow Bernadette in line with this new concept. She was right about one thing. He had wanted to be first. He wanted to be the husband and father of a Christ-centered home, just like Eli, and he'd endured a considerable amount of spiritual discipline to keep himself pure for that future virgin bride.

From the moment he laid eyes on Bernadette, he'd hoped she was the one.

Had it just been a year and a half ago? He and Eli had taken on that singles project with their church, delivering toys and clothing to the orphanage. He'd walked into Niños de Cristos to find her in the kitchen, supervising peanut butter sandwich construction while simultaneously listening to an elephant joke and bandaging a skinned knee.

Barefoot under one of those gauzy skirts, black hair spiraling like live silk, a welcoming smile had lit that dark-flower face. And when she'd laughed, husky and unexpectedly deep, his knees turned to jelly.

Eli gave him a hard time about hopeless cases all the way home. But he could take everything his brother dished out, and he was willing to be patient with Bernadette. She was worth the wait.

He lowered the camera and watched her with his heart instead of the objective camera lens. He still saw purity. He still saw incandescent kindness and deep spirituality.

She was the one. He just had to make her see it, too.

EIGHT

Heading north toward Ciudad Victoria, Briggs swiped a hand across his scratchy two-day beard. He couldn't wait to get to a hotel where he could get a meal, brush his teeth and take a shower. Plus, his head hurt so bad he could hardly stay on the road. Nearly drove right into one of the garlic stands that lined the highway.

When he caught up with this girl, he was going to make her pay for his inconvenience. Kill her lover, too. Right in front of her.

The thought made him feel marginally better. Revenge would be so sweet, he wouldn't even charge the judge extra for the double hit.

After leaving Poza Rica, he'd driven north toward Ciudad Victoria, looking for the blue Dodge. He'd almost missed it abandoned on the side of the road in the dark. Cursing, he doubled back and got out to make sure that was it.

It was, and they were gone.

Well, at least he knew where they were headed. A little ways further, he'd passed a bunch of Mexican fruit

Gypsies camped on the side of the road. He'd stopped to ask if they'd seen the girl and the cop, but when he opened the car door, a wild boar had appeared in his headlights, snorting and threatening to charge. So he got back in and drove on.

He'd find them when they got to Victoria City.

Benny woke up when a rooster crowed beneath the bed of the truck in which she'd slept alongside Marta and Reyna. She sat up and rubbed her eyes. *Talk about getting up with the chickens...*

Owen had spent the night under the tent extension, rolled up on a quilt beside little Jefe, with Noé and Ana Maria on an air mattress nearby.

Benny peered over the side and found him crouched on the ground, brushing his teeth with the contents of a bottle of water. He looked up and grinned around his toothbrush, then spat and rinsed his mouth.

"Good mornin', sunshine." He sneezed, then sneezed again and again, five times in all.

"Wow, that was impressive. Bless you."

"Don't know what makes me do that. Sometimes it's eight or ten times before I quit."

"That's the weirdest thing I've ever heard of."

"Then you don't get out much." He smiled and rose. "If you're hungry, Ana Maria has tortillas and fruit for breakfast."

Benny located the source of the smoke and delicious smells in a little cast-iron cooker over a campfire. The entire Fronteras family had gathered around it, leaving her asleep. Amazing that the laughter, singing and loud, affectionate disagreement hadn't woken her up. She must have been more tired than she'd thought.

"*El baño*'s thataway." Owen aimed a thumb at a stand of trees a few yards off the road, then sauntered toward the campfire.

When she sat down beside him a few minutes later, he reached over to pluck a couple of oranges out of a basket. Slicing off the tops with his knife, he handed her one, along with a smile. "You sleep okay?"

"Like the proverbial rock." Feeling inexplicably shy, she sucked the juice out of the orange, delighting in its fresh sweetness. Better than anything she'd had in the States. She glanced at the backpack between Owen's feet. "I don't suppose you have a comb in there, do you?"

"Ask and ye shall receive." He rooted around in his backpack and produced a small plastic comb. At least it was clean. He'd apparently already used it; his black hair was still wet, smoothed back from his face.

"Thanks." Tossing the orange rind into the fire, she combed out snarls and listened to Owen tease Jefe about the cartoon mermaid on his T-shirt. By the time she'd finished plaiting her hair into a French braid, Ana Maria was wrapping a warm tortilla around a banana for her breakfast. Smiling, the older woman handed it to her, along with a handful of animal crackers.

Benny bit the head off a rhinoceros and chased it with a swallow of Owen's bottled water. The banana was firm and ripe, and the tortilla's lovely roasted-corn flavor eased the pinch of her stomach. Completely at peace, she sat with her elbows on her knees and ate her fill. She smiled as Reyna pulled Owen to his feet. They danced a silly, innocent version of the "Macarena" as Jefe kept time on the bottom of an aluminum pot.

"Where are you going, my dears?" asked Marta as Benny finished the last of her cookies. "Is this a wedding journey?"

"No, señora." Why did everyone assume they were honeymooners? Was there something in her face that she hadn't put there? She hoped Owen hadn't heard the question. She felt a blush climb her neck. "We're just friends—traveling companions headed back to the U.S. There was an accident with our plane and we had to go down just north of Veracruz."

"Ayi." Marta vigorously scrubbed the skillet with sand. "What a terrible thing! It is because of the good God that you are alive, eh?"

"Indeed it is." Benny reached out to touch the crucifix on a leather string around the woman's wrinkled neck. "God has had His hand on us for the last two days." She paused. "Do you know Him?"

"Yes, my daughter. He is my Father and my Friend. I saw in your faces that you belong to Him. I told Noé that it would be good to take you in."

"Mama Marta is wiser than many libraries full of books." Ana Maria took the skillet and wiped it briskly with a clean cloth. "She thinks you will bring us good luck. We will sell many oranges and get a big price for the bananas."

Benny laughed. "I don't know about that, but if you have room for us, we'll work hard in whatever way we can. How far are you going?"

"Ciudad Victoria is less than an hour away." Noé, engaged in pulling up a tent stob, looked over his shoulder. "We'll stop there for water and gas, then go on to the border at Reynosa."

Benny clapped her hands. "Wonderful! When can we go?"

"As soon as we pack the tent."

Owen helped roll up the tent, pack the poles and store the camping supplies in the truck. He laughed until he cried, watching Ana Maria coax fat Fernanda into her trailer by placing hunks of banana, one at a time, along a ramp composed of two stout planks. He wondered if the pig would have been so greedy if she'd known she was headed for her execution.

Noé, Ana Maria and Marta piled into the cab of the truck. Two chickens, the rooster and the fruit filled the back, except for a tight corner near the cab, where Benny wedged herself with the two children. Owen, perched on top of a wooden crate, negotiated Jefe and Reyna's squabble over who would get to sit in Benny's lap. Jefe, younger but of far stronger personality, wound up in the seat of honor, with Reyna and her doll snuggled under Benny's arm.

The little boy reached up to finger the braid hanging over Benny's shoulder, pulling its curly end through his fingers. He was a skinny, bright-eyed child, tongue loose at both ends, and his black hair stuck up in a rooster tail on the back of his head. Reminded Owen a lot of his nephew, Danilo.

Benny must have been thinking the same thing. "Did Eli mention Isabel and the kids when you talked to him yesterday?"

"Nope. Too busy yelling at me for not calling sooner.

And for not filing a flight plan. And for breathing." He laughed. "You responsible people should cut us ADHD folks some slack."

"Maybe you're used to thinking of yourself that way, but you're just a little impulsive." She gently touched Jefe's cheek. He'd fallen asleep with his head on Bernadette's shoulder. "After all, you made it through college and you're good at your job."

He flushed, pleased at her praise. Her opinion meant a lot. "I did fine at Baylor once I got to the courses I liked." He laughed. "Freshman comp nearly did me in."

She smiled. "I used to be pretty impulsive myself."

"No way."

"I had to learn the hard way."

"The hard way?"

"When I was about thirteen—fourteen, maybe—I remember feeling like a bird caught in a tornado. When you don't have any control over your life, you beat against the wind, trying to get it back."

"So what made you change?"

"Well, once I settled in with people who cared enough to give me boundaries, I was able to focus on long-term goals." She looked at him, eyes intense, hugging the two children in her arms. "You can do anything if you have hope."

"I suppose." As they entered the Ciudad Victoria city limits, the truck jounced over a *tope,* a speed bump. Owen grabbed the nearest crate and hung on for dear life. "I don't think I've ever had long-term goals, beyond moving up in the Agency."

"Doing a job you love is a fine ambition. Plus, you

have your Mission Aviation Fellowship flights." She tilted her head. "Aren't you satisfied with that?"

"Satisfied? Yeah, but since Eli and Isabel moved to San Antonio, I just have my mom and myself to look out for. And Mom's pretty independent. I confess, it gets a little lonely sometimes." *Now where'd that come from?* Until the words came out of his mouth, he hadn't acknowledged their truth. He leaned over, forearms on his knees, so that he could talk to Bernadette without yelling against the wind. "I told you, I'm a closet homebody."

She looked thoughtful. "I know what you mean, even though I really like to travel. I'm happy for Meg and Jack, of course, but I miss her companionship. That's part of being human—you know, wanting to connect with somebody who loves you no matter what."

So she got it. Something warm bloomed under his rib cage. What would it be like to be able to communicate this way all the time? Being raised by a man's man like Dennis Carmichael wasn't exactly conducive to exploring the tender side of one's character. And stoicism was a hallmark of the Border Patrol profession. He'd developed a habit of clowning around to cover his feelings. Maybe without even realizing it.

Bernadette didn't mind laughing at his teasing, but she never treated him as a lightweight. Which, in a backward sort of way, made him feel stronger.

He put his chin on his fist and studied her for a moment. Her gaze was on the black splash of Jefe's eyelashes, but she looked up and their eyes held.

She knew. He didn't know how, but she did. Had he really imagined he could hide his feelings?

"So how are Isabel's classes going?" She looked away, voice studiously bright. "Last time I talked to her, she was planning to take fifteen hours this semester."

He sighed. She wasn't going to acknowledge what was between them. Probably just as well. Reyna had tired of her doll and was playing with Bernadette's silver-and-turquoise ring. The little girl probably didn't know much English, but you never knew what small ears would pick up.

"Oh, Isabel. She's got a 4.0, naturally. Eli has seriously outmarried himself."

Bernadette laughed. "They're perfect for each other. I was afraid he was never going to get around to asking her to marry him."

"Might not have if that thug Medeiros hadn't gone on his vendetta."

"Taking on the U.S. Border Patrol wasn't his smartest move, was it?"

"He'll be in the slammer for the rest of his life." He paused. "And when I find out who shot down my plane, he's gonna wish he'd busted into somebody else's school yard."

The fact that he felt a lot more possessive and protective about Bernadette than about the plane was information he'd probably better keep to himself.

Holding Reyna by the hand, Benny stopped to examine an array of brightly colored scarves displayed on a wooden table in one of the many open-air booths that comprised the *mercado* in Ciudad Victoria's downtown Plaza Hidalgo.

They'd had a quick but filling meal prepared by the

women at the campground. Then Noé, Ana Maria and
Marta had retired for a siesta. Owen and Benny had
taken the children to the market.

On a sleepy afternoon there were few shoppers, and
the atmosphere was relaxed. Trays of colorful fruits and
vegetables alternated with dry-goods displays, and
beautiful historical murals adorned the walls of mu-
seums and theaters. It was a city where the modern
bumped up against the ancient with charm and artistic
flair. A storefront window featuring a statue of the
Virgin of Guadalupe briefly caught their attention
before they moved on to the scarf booth.

"Look, Reyna. Let's try this on you." Benny plucked
a silky red-and-orange length of fabric from the pile on
the table and draped it around the little girl's head.
Smiling, the woman behind the table picked up a hand
mirror and held it for Reyna to look.

Reyna preened and grinned, her perfect white teeth
gleaming. The bright stripes of the scarf contrasted with
the ebony sheen of her hair and made onyx gems of her
eyes. "My papa will buy this for me if I ask just so." She
tipped her head and artfully pouted her bottom lip, eyes
sparkling with mischief.

Benny laughed. "I think, sweet baby, you are going
to break some hearts one day."

"I'd say that's a given." Owen had crossed the narrow
street with Jefe trotting at his heels. Each had a sugar-
dusted curl of fried dough on a stick and a multicolored
lollipop.

"Ooh, I want one of those." Reyna pointed at Jefe's
candy.

"Here, have this one." Owen handed her his wrapped

sucker and gave the bread stick to Benny. "Too much grease and sugar for my taste."

Benny bit into the crusty pastry and closed her eyes in ecstasy. "Mmm. What's not to like?"

"Give me a jalapeño popper any day."

"I like those, too." Benny took another nibble, savoring the sweetness. "Come on, let's go over to that—" She stopped dead, nearly dropping the bread stick.

Owen caught her by the shoulders to keep from running over her. "What's the matter?"

"Did you see that guy?" she said in English. No need to alarm the children.

Shading his eyes against the glare of the sun off hard-baked streets and whitewashed buildings, Owen peered over her shoulder. "What guy? Where?"

"He just went between those two jewelry stalls at the end of the square."

"I didn't notice anybody. What did he look like?"

"Heavy shoulders, black sunglasses and a big nose. Dark skin, but he looked more Italian than Latino."

"What was he wearing?"

Benny felt her heart pumping harder by the second. Gripping Reyna's hand, she took Jefe by the elbow and pulled them toward the campsite. "Come on, we've got to get out of here."

Owen followed, looking over his shoulder. "Did you recognize him? Was it the guy who shot at you?"

"I'm not sure." She didn't want to slow down to find out. "He had on navy-blue pants like my shooter did but not the jacket and tie. It might have been him." By now, she was panting, running down the side street they'd taken to the market.

Owen picked up Jefe and ran with him. "Last one back to the truck has to give Fernanda a kiss," he said in Spanish.

Clutching Benny's hand, Reyna looked up, brows puckered.

Benny gave the little girl a reassuring smile. "Come on, we can't let the boys win." They were running flat out now.

Glancing back, she didn't see Mr. Big Nose, and Owen stayed between her and the street. But she couldn't help the tremors that shook her body.

Could that really have been the shooter? How could he have tracked them down so fast? Maybe deep down she'd feared he would eventually find her. She shouldn't have let Owen talk her into eating at that restaurant. Too many people had seen them.

Mexico was a big place, but a man who could locate her on the Yucatán, even after she'd changed her name, could do it again.

Finally. The truck was in sight. The two children ran ahead to the tent.

"Mama!" shouted Jefe. "I won! Reyna has to kiss the pig!"

But Reyna was right on his heels. "I do not! Fernanda has bad breath."

"Wait, Benny." Owen grabbed her arm and pulled her behind an RV two spaces down from the Fronterases' truck. He was barely breathing hard, though her lungs were bursting from fear. "Who was the guy you saw?"

"I'm not sure. Maybe nobody." She leaned against the door, sucking in air. "I'm probably spooked over nothing. A shadow."

"Bernadette." Owen searched her face, brows drawn

together. "Come on. So he had on the navy-blue pants. What color was his shirt?"

"White. Or maybe light blue. I'm not sure." She put her hands over her face.

"Calm down." Owen lowered his voice, gently rubbing his hands up and down her arms. "All right, say this is the guy...our shooter. Did he see you?"

"I don't think so. Like I said, he went down that alley. If he'd seen me, he would have followed, right?" What did she know about hit men?

"Probably. Give me every detail you can. Better yet, could you draw a picture?"

"Owen!" Benny gave a shaky laugh. "I don't sing, I don't dance and I certainly don't draw. Meg was the artist."

"Okay, then just describe him as best you can. Start with height and weight."

"C-can we sit down? My legs feel like spaghetti."

"I'm sorry. Sure." He let go of her shoulders and they both dropped onto the grass in front of the camper.

She leaned over, arms crossed over her middle. Closing her eyes, she could feel all over again the stunned realization that a bullet had just whizzed over the top of her head and planted itself in the wall of the building. It could have killed her or one of the women still in the dormitory.

Her stomach lurched.

She felt Owen slide closer. His knees didn't quite touch hers, but she could feel the strength of his presence, his comfort. "Are you all right?"

She took a deep breath. "I'm just thinking. He was about five foot ten and weighed about two hundred pounds. Solid muscle. Like I said, big, thick shoulders and long arms." She closed her eyes in thought. "His hair was getting a little thin on top, one of those hairlines that recede at the sides. He wasn't an ugly guy, just…hard faced, you know?" She looked at Owen and he nodded.

"How would you describe the shape of his face? Any complexion abnormalities?"

"Oh!" She sat up a little. "He did have a rough complexion, like maybe he'd recently had a skin peel. Square jaw and a slight cleft in his chin."

"And you said he looked Italian?"

"Yes. That olive skin tone, thick black brows and really dark eyes."

Owen bumped his thumbs together. "Wow. Going to be a little hard to pick him out in a country where ninety percent of the population fits that description."

A short silence fell, and Benny wished she had something more descriptive to say about her attacker. "The only time I saw him close up was when he came to the clinic to interview me."

"When was that?"

"Tuesday afternoon. The day before we left. I was holding babies while Dr. Wes gave inoculations. There was a mother who wanted me to take her baby back to the States. To keep it. They do that sometimes and it's so hard…."

His knees pressed against the outside of hers. "I know, Benny."

Opening her eyes, she met his gaze. Electric awareness passed between them. This morning in the truck she'd almost told him about that year in Memphis. The year she'd sold herself, body and soul.

Looking down at Owen's big, callused hands, loosely

linked between his knees, she clutched her fingers together to keep from reaching out to him.

"Anyway, he came right into the clinic, ignoring all those people standing in line. Like they weren't worth beans. And he insisted on talking to me, even though there were babies screaming and that long line—" She gulped down a fresh wave of anger. "So I went outside with him."

"What did he want?"

"He said he was FBI and he had reason to believe someone had a contract on me. He wanted me to come back to the States with him right then."

"A contract." Owen's hands clenched. "Bernadette, this is not normal. Come on, look at me."

He would want to touch her, hold her hands, and she couldn't give in to that weakness. But she was so tired. So afraid.

NINE

Owen had years of experience questioning illegal aliens who slipped across the border and got stranded in the Texas desert by their coyotes. But getting a simple explanation out of one small American woman was proving to be beyond his capabilities.

He sat very still, watching Bernadette struggle, wishing he could see inside her head, wanting to deliver her. Maybe that was the key. Nobody but God Himself could right whatever was wrong.

But Lord! I'm involved up to my eyeballs. Why did You let me fall for her and then find out she's being chased by a hit man?

Slowly, as if completely against her will, Benny's heavy, exotic eyelids lifted and bang, he was sucked into her pain. He knew she'd made her decision. She wasn't letting him in. Fear had won.

And the worst thing was, she was more afraid of *his knowledge* than of dying.

"Don't, Benny. Don't do this."

She pressed her lips together, gave a tiny shake of her head. "I'm not doing anything."

"Yes, you are. You're closing up again, and I—" he couldn't help reaching for her hands "—I don't want to go back."

But she slid her fingers free and stood. "We're not going back. We're going to see if the Fronterases are ready to go, and we'll head for the border with them."

He got to his feet, feeling like the ground had shifted beneath him. "But what if that guy—"

"We'll outrun him again. Come on, help me find a phone. I've decided I've got to call Meg after all. She—she won't be surprised at what's happened."

That stopped him. "Benny... I have to tell you something, and you're not gonna like it."

She stiffened. "What have you done?"

"I already told Eli to call Meg and Jack."

"You did *what?*" Red flags went up in her cheekbones. "Owen, this is my personal business—"

"Yeah, but I'm pretty involved, wouldn't you say?" He lifted his hands. "Somebody has to know what's going on in order to help us when we get to the States."

"I can't believe you did that without telling me!"

"Feels pretty rotten to get left out of the loop, doesn't it?"

At an impasse, they stared at one another. Bernadette looked away first. "I told you a long time ago you didn't want to get involved with me."

"Yeah, well, I don't like being told what to do."

She laughed, short and hard. "I guess control is the issue, isn't it?"

"Right now, our *lives* are the issue. If you'll tell me who we're running from and what you're trying to accomplish, I can be a help instead of a big lump who keeps getting in the way."

Her eyes flashed to his. "You're not a lump! And you're not in the way."

But clearly she wasn't going to tell him anything more. He was getting really tired of the runaround. "Let's just get back to the States as fast as we can. You can use my cell phone to call whoever you want to. I've been saving it for emergencies."

"I'd say emergencies R us." Bernadette gave him an unhappy look.

"Yeah, whatever." He turned and headed for Noé's truck, but couldn't quite make himself leave her behind. He looked over his shoulder to make sure she followed.

One day chivalry was going to get him killed.

Stacy Garrett sat down on Bernadette's bottom bunk bed in the women's dormitory at the Agrexco mission. It was still made with military precision, the pillow smooth as glass and the items on the camp stool beside the bed arranged in a perfect square. Hairbrush, mirror, glasses, toiletries in a one-gallon Ziploc bag. As far as Stacy could tell, there was nothing missing.

Except Benny herself.

In the brief time the young woman was here in Agrexco, the two of them had gotten surprisingly close. Benny was a huge help in the clinic—more than a translator, she would set her hand to anything that needed doing. And it was nice to have another woman to talk to, even if Benny was private about her personal life. What fun to see the way Owen Carmichael had looked at her. But Benny had been gone for three days now, without a word. No matter what Wes said about minding her own business, Stacy was going to do some poking around.

She got down on her knees and pulled the suitcase out from under the bed. That was just one of the weird things about this whole situation. Why had Benny left without her clothes? Maybe there was something in here that would shed some light on what was going on.

Concern for Benny warred with guilt about snooping as she unzipped the suitcase and opened it. As expected, the cotton skirts and knit tops were packed in neat rolls for minimum creasing. But what grabbed Stacy's immediate attention was the cell phone lying right on top.

She picked up the phone. Cellular reception here was spotty. There was a regular landline phone in the village ten miles away, but after the hurricane, even that was unreliable.

She sat there with her thumbnail in her mouth. Going through the numbers stored in Benny's cell phone seemed presumptuous. How would she know who to call?

Lord, what should I do?

The sensible thing seemed to be to start with the missions agency. She and Wes were career missionaries here in Agrexco, while Benny was on short-term loan from the orphanage in Acuña. They all worked for the same agency that had arranged for Owen to bring their supplies.

But what could she tell them, beyond the fact that Benny and Owen had left the village ahead of schedule? It would make Benny look bad, when there was probably a reasonable explanation for her behavior. Stacy frowned. If only she knew what that reasonable explanation was!

Before she could talk herself out of it, she flipped

open the phone and searched for received calls. The most recent call was from an unknown ID, but Stacy immediately recognized the area code. The same as her mother-in-law's. One of the things that had instantly drawn her and Benny together had been a common familiarity with the southwest corner of Tennessee.

But Benny had said she never went back there, hadn't been back since her teens.

Stacy pushed the call button. This was crazy, but she had to know what had happened to Benny. Maybe the last person she'd talked to could shed some light—

"Hello?" It was a dark, smoky female voice. In just that one word, Stacy heard caution, maybe fear. "Bernadette, where are you?"

"Hi, my name's Stacy Garrett and I'm calling for Benny—Bernadette, I mean?" She had no idea what to say, making it up as she went along.

"What? Why do you have her phone?" Now the slow voice was tight with suspicion.

Afraid the woman might hang up, Stacy said hurriedly, "I'm her friend, a missionary to Mexico. It's kind of a strange situation, but Benny's disappeared and I thought you might know what happened to her."

"*Disappeared?* What do you mean?"

"I'll explain but—" Stacy swallowed "—first I have to know who you are. I'm worried about her."

"I'm Ladonna. Ladonna Sherman. Did she get away before he got to her?"

"Who?" Stacy was afraid she'd gotten hold of a madwoman. "Was somebody trying to hurt Benny?"

"You better believe it, lady. Now start over and tell me exactly what happened."

Chilled, Stacy clutched the phone until it hurt her hand. *Deep breaths, Stace. You asked for this.* Quickly she explained the events of the last few days. Unfortunately, what she knew was sketchy at best. "And I haven't heard from her or Owen in two days," she finished.

"I was afraid of—" The rest of the woman's sentence was drowned in static.

"Ms. Sherman?" Dismayed, Stacy looked at the phone display. The call had failed. "Oh, no," she whispered. "Poor Benny."

Owen's tight-lipped attitude took Benny completely off guard. Not that he verbally raged—or, for that matter, behaved in any way other than with his usual sterling courtesy. But the sunshine had definitely gone behind a cloud. He accompanied her back to the Fronterases' truck, where he locked up the backpack, retrieved his cell phone and handed it to her without a word. Then he turned on his heel and left her to her privacy.

That was what she'd wanted. Wasn't it?

She climbed into the truck with the phone and sat on the broad passenger seat with her feet drawn up. Her sandals had rubbed painful blisters on both insteps, and Owen's jeans had begun to wear at the knees. Not having had a bath in two days, she probably smelled like Fernanda's cage, too. She was just a mess, physically and emotionally. It was a wonder Owen was willing to stay with her, much less not get upset when she wouldn't talk to him.

Putting her head down on her knees, she spent a few minutes in prayer. Thanked God for His protection so far. Asked for wisdom and help. Confessed her fear and anxiety.

Last year, when one of her kids at the orphanage had been murdered by the same drug smuggler who'd kidnapped Isabel and Danilo and traumatized Mercedes, it had really shaken her faith. Which was ridiculous. She'd been in bad fixes before. Sometimes, when she was drifting off to sleep, her mind would replay the events that had brought her away from Beale Street. From nightmare to fantasy in just a few days.

Owen thought she was such a snow maiden. If he knew the things she'd done, the battles she'd fought to escape it all, he wouldn't be so persistent in pursuing her. That was why she couldn't tell him. She admitted, just between her and the Lord, that Owen Carmichael's regard meant more to her than safety.

The Lord could protect her without Owen's help. He'd promised to do so. Phrases from Psalm 18 passed through her mind on a flood of joy.

I love you, O Lord, my strength. The Lord is my rock, my fortress and my deliverer; my God is my rock, in whom I take refuge. He is my shield and the horn of my salvation, my stronghold. I call to the Lord, who is worthy of praise, and I am saved from my enemies.

Yes, she was going to be fine. One way or another. If the Lord took her home to Heaven early, what better place could she be? No reason to be afraid.

Still, a tiny corner of her heart wished there was a

way to connect with a helpmate. Being with Owen twenty-four hours a day had made that little desire grow larger by the hour.

Lord, don't make me long for things I can't have. I beg You to remove this awful yearning for something other than You. I want to be completely set apart for You alone.

That had to be the right thing to ask for.

She looked at the phone clutched in her hand. Owen's phone. He'd saved it for her use. Waited until she asked for it and given it up without question. She flipped it open and smiled at the photo on the screen. A close-up of his horse. At least, she assumed it was his—a beautiful roan with a cream-colored mane and blaze and intelligent dark eyes.

She had just keyed in the number of her supervisor at the mission agency when the door beside her suddenly swung open.

"Owen! What are you doing?"

"Benny, we're leaving!"

"Why? What's the matter?"

"Your stalker found you. He's out there by the road talking to Marta. She'll keep him busy while we haul our buns outta here. Come *on,* I said!"

Benny scrambled out of the truck, stuffing the phone into her pocket. She followed Owen's example of ducking and dodging the RVs, pop-up campers and American family cars crammed into the big campground. She struggled to keep up with Owen's long legs and he grabbed her hand.

"Come on, babe, you can do it! Run!"

Benny found herself being towed toward the opposite

side of the lot, where a six-foot chain-link fence separated the campground from the street. "What's he doing?" She was too frightened to look.

"Oh, man, he's got a gun out now!" Owen shunted around a Winnebago at the end of the row.

"Maybe we should go back and— Ow!" Benny had bruised her hip on the RV's bumper. "How are we going to get over the fence?"

"Climb."

"But I can't—"

"I'll help you. You want to get shot at again?"

"I'd rather not." The fence loomed. Benny made the mistake of looking back. Mr. Big Nose had spotted them. He was charging after them, a cell phone pressed to his ear. At least he couldn't shoot them until he put down the phone.

"You'd rather not climb the fence or you'd rather not get shot?" Without waiting for an answer, Owen bent and cupped his hands. "Up you go."

Sandals weren't the ideal climbing shoe, but bare feet would have been worse. Benny let Owen boost her halfway up the fence. She grabbed the top and heaved herself upward, cutting her hands on the sharp points. Feet scrabbling for toeholds, she climbed until she hung over the top rail. Dizzy with fear, she felt the fence jerk and clang as Owen climbed up beside her.

"Come on, you can do it. Leg over." He was already vaulting across. Landing on the other side, he reached up for her. "Bernadette, I'll catch you."

She looked over her shoulder again. The hit man had put the phone away. The gun was at his shoulder.

"Please, God, help!" Ignoring the pain in her hands and the cuts on her stomach, she slung her right leg over the top of the fence. Owen grabbed her foot.

"Good girl. Now the other one. I won't let you fall."

Closing her eyes, she put her weight into Owen's palm and kicked the other leg across.

Just as she dropped into his arms, a shot rang out. A bullet whizzed across the top of the fence. Benny screamed, throwing her arms around Owen's neck.

He snatched her close for a second, then set her on her feet. "Come on!"

They were on the street between the campground and the Ciudad Victoria bus station, which squatted in front of a blue-and-white water tower. Dashing across the street, they ran for the cinderblock wall around the bus station. Benny looked back. The hit man was nowhere in sight; apparently, he'd been stopped by the fence.

The perimeter of the wall was lackadaisically landscaped with a few skinny cottonwood trees, which they dodged as they ran. They reached the first corner without seeing an opening. A hundred yards or so farther down, they skidded around another corner.

Benny nearly sobbed in relief when she saw the bus station's green entrance awning. "Will we be safe in here?"

Owen didn't slow down. "I'm guessing he won't expect us to head indoors." He suddenly stopped under the awning, swinging her against his chest. "By the way—" he was breathing normally, though Benny was gasping for air "—you were right about big cities. Are you sure you don't want to go to the Mexican police?"

"I don't trust anybody here."

Owen nodded. "Okay then. We'll catch a bus to the border and we should be home free." He shoved open the glass door and pulled her into the bus station.

Taking a shot at the girl in broad daylight, in a campground full of tourists and fruit vendors, had been a dumb, impulsive move. Now Ray was going to have to pay for it.

The old lady had started yelling for the police and he'd had to make a run for it.

It was the judge's fault for calling to check in with him in the middle of the interrogation. He'd been so startled by the sight of his quarry right there in plain sight, he'd completely lost his head. Cutting the judge off in midsentence, he'd taken aim and fired.

Now here he was, driving like a lunatic through the streets of Ciudad Victoria, trying to guess where an American border cop and a missionary ex-hooker would go in a foreign country. They were headed back to the States, of course, but how would they get there?

TEN

Standing in line at the ticket counter, Owen looked over his shoulder at Benny. She sat on a wooden bench in a corner, next to a tiny Native American woman who clutched a galvanized bucket to her chest. Naturally, they were carrying on an animated discussion. Benny smiled her megawatt smile and peered into the bucket, admiring some undisclosed item. She was something else.

He would have given anything to have back the money he had spent on that little blue car. Benny had been right about almost everything since they'd started this odyssey.

Stay out of big cities.

Don't spend all the cash.

Using the credit card had been a big mistake, too. How else had the guy found them, except by tracing them to the restaurant in Poza Rica?

At least he was finally heeding her advice about taking a bus to the border. He just hoped they could get on it in time to avoid their pursuer.

When his turn came at last, he stepped up to the counter. "Two tickets to Reynosa," he said in Spanish.

"That bus left ten minutes ago, señor. I'm sorry. The next one is at six this afternoon."

He slapped down his Visa card. Didn't matter if they used the credit card now. By the time the guy traced this expenditure, he and Benny would be safely across the border. "It hasn't left yet. It's sitting right out there and I'm getting on it. Give me the tickets." He smiled. "Please hurry."

"Señor, the bus is full—"

"We'll stand in the aisle if we have to. Charge me double fare! I don't care. Just hurry!"

The clerk, who looked like he'd been up for twenty-four hours at least, glanced pointedly at the line of people behind Owen. "The next bus to Reynosa is at six," he repeated.

Owen leaned in. "You see that young lady over there in the corner?"

The clerk stood on his tiptoes and peered over Owen's shoulder. *"Sí."*

"That's my new wife. We're on our honeymoon, and we just got word she has to get home for a funeral to-morrow morning." And it was probably going to be *his* funeral if she found out he'd made up such a whopper.

Lord, it's an emergency, he excused himself, when his conscience jabbed him. *And she did say she had to get to a funeral.*

The ticket agent's expression softened as Berna-dette took one of the old woman's arthritic hands and held it to her own blooming cheek. She kissed the knobby fingers and closed her eyes, murmuring in obvious prayer.

With a sigh, the agent took Owen's Visa card and

ran it through the credit machine. "Don't blame me if you miss it."

"Thanks." Shifting with impatience, Owen kept an eye on the bus through the open terminal door. He heard the engine grumble to life as the clerk gave him a receipt to sign. After turning it upside down to scrawl his name, he snatched the tickets and ran. "Benny! Come on, let's go!" The bus driver was shutting the door.

Benny looked up. "You mean right now?"

"Yes, right now."

She dropped the elderly woman's hand and rose with a respectful smile. *"Adiós, abuela. Vaya con Dios."*

Owen danced with impatience. "We're gonna miss the bus! Come on!" He grabbed Benny's elbow and pulled her out the door. They pelted toward the bus, where Owen banged on the door with the flat of his hand. "Open up!" He held up the tickets. "Let us in!"

The driver peered through the window in the door for an agonizing moment, then reluctantly opened it. *"No cabe nadie más, señor."* We are full.

"Tenemos los boletos," Owen said, boosting Benny up the steps. We have tickets.

"Lo siento, señor, pero—"

Suddenly, a commotion ensued from the back of the bus—noisy squawks accompanied by flapping wings. Everyone on the bus turned to look.

A red-faced Anglo couple stood up and stumbled down the aisle, lugging a huge birdcage between them. It contained a pair of brilliantly colored parrots, evidently the source of the uproar. "Sorry, sorry, *con permiso, perdón,"* the man muttered as he and his companion banged into people sitting along the aisle.

They stopped to address the driver. "Just realized we left the bird's papers at the hotel. They won't let us across the border without them."

When the driver looked blank, Owen interpreted.

"Van a tomarles los asientos," growled the driver. You'll lose your seats.

Owen could hardly contain a victory dance. He met Benny's twinkling eyes. "Guess we get a ride after all, huh?"

Briggs screeched into the bus station parking lot on two badly damaged wheels. He'd hit a monster-size pothole on the way from the campground and heard a sickening pop and hiss.

He couldn't have said when it occurred to him that the bus station was the obvious place to look for them; it was just a finely tuned intuition. But he was going to have to hurry. He'd fired a gun in a public campground and he could already hear sirens in the background. If they caught up to him, he'd have to jump through all kinds of hoops to excuse his outrageous behavior. If the judge had to get involved, he was not going to be a happy camper.

But "sufficient to the day is the evil thereof" was what his grandma used to say when she was telling him not to borrow trouble. Whatever that meant.

Anyway, one problem at a time.

He abandoned the Crown Victoria—interesting co-incidence that his car and the town had the same name—and raced inside the station. Wildly, he looked around but didn't see hide nor hair of his quarry. He chugged past the line of people waiting for tickets, shoved aside a fat-lady tourist wearing the ugliest hat he'd ever seen and slapped a hand on the counter.

"*¡Americanos!* Have you seen two of them?" He held up two fingers.

The ticket agent copied his move. "Peace. *Es necesario esperar,* señor." Wait.

"No! Not peace! Two! *Dos* Americans!" He didn't have time to dig out his phrase book, so he raised his voice and spoke slowly. "A man and a woman dressed like a little boy. Did they buy tickets just now?"

The lady he'd pushed aside tapped him on the shoulder. "There were two Americans in here a little while ago, but they just got on that bus." She jerked a thumb toward the open doorway, where he saw a bus huffing and steaming. It began to move, spewing exhaust. "Now would you get to the end of the line where you belong, you jerk? It's my turn."

Briggs stepped on her toe hard as he tore outside. But he was too late. The bus pulled away before he reached the curb. Boiling with frustration, he ran behind it, breathing exhaust fumes for half a block before his asthma kicked in. Wheezing, he slowed, then stopped in the middle of the street, doubled over. A motorcycle roared past, then another bus, honking at him.

He'd let them get away again. One minute earlier and he'd have had them. He was going to be shaking hands with Frank Carter in Hades if he didn't get this thing in gear soon.

Trudging back inside the terminal, he ignored the woman in the ugly hat, who gave him a dirty look as he went by. He scanned the schedule posted above the ticket window. The bus was headed to Reynosa, at least he knew that much. He could drive hard and fast, get there first and nail both of them as they got off the bus.

It was going to be a pleasure to take them out.

"Okay, I've got to know what was in that bucket."

Benny leaned back against the seat, limp now that the adrenaline of running for the bus had drained away. They were on their way to Reynosa.

She rolled her head to look at Owen. "What bucket?"

"The lady you were talking to at the bus station. What did she have in that thing?"

"Oh, just stuff. A coffee mug. A pair of slippers. A dress and a necklace. Everything she had in the world."

"Where was she going?"

"To Rio Bravo to live with her daughter. Her husband just died."

"How do you do that? Get stuff out of people without even trying? You'd make a great Border Patrol agent."

"I don't think so." The very idea annoyed her. "I wouldn't like sending people back to live in some of the places I've seen."

"Bernadette, I've seen those places, too. But I've also helicoptered people out of the desert—dehydrated, sick, broken bones, snakebitten."

"I know." Contrite, she touched his wrist. "I wasn't being critical of you or the Border Patrol. I understand your job, and I appreciate it. It's just that people like that little woman make me so sad."

He turned his hand and caught hers before she could snatch it away. She instinctively tugged for a second, then gave in. How could she feel so torn about something as simple as touching hands? The connection, skin to skin, comforted and frightened her in nearly equal degrees. He laced his fingers through hers, spreading them to fit, until the roughness of his palm lay against hers.

She made herself relax. "Aren't you still angry with me?"

"Nope." She looked at him, but his eyes were closed, his big body relaxed into the frayed gray upholstery of the seat. "I wish you'd talk to me, but anger takes too much energy."

"You've got enough energy for three people." But she couldn't help smiling.

"I saw you praying with that lady. Do you know we've never prayed together?"

"Yes, we have. In church—"

"Church doesn't count. All those other people there— God bless the missionaries, help so-and-so in the hospital, et cetera. No. All our narrow escapes from death and destruction and we've never prayed, just you and me."

"Do you want to?"

He turned his head, opened his eyes, and the sleepy, latent expression there made her brain swim. "I do. Can I lead?"

She nodded. Even as she closed her eyes, the metaphor struck her hard. She'd been in charge of her own life for so long that letting go of it took an enormous step of faith. As she listened to Owen talk to God, very simply and directly, her resistance to him cracked another notch.

He prayed for each one of the Mexican nationals they'd met on their journey so far: Mariela and Gustavo, Jorge at the car lot, the schoolteacher by the outhouse, the Fronteras family, even the *federal* who'd searched them for drugs. But when he started praying for the hit man, she froze.

"Owen, don't do that."

"Huh?" He opened his eyes. "Best thing that could happen is for this guy to have a change of heart."

"I know that but I can't…" Ashamed, she stopped and swallowed. "Never mind, go ahead."

He squeezed her hand and clasped it between both of his. "I'm not asking you to. But I need to. Otherwise, I get too focused on getting back at him."

"I understand." She waited and Owen bowed his head again.

"Lord, please help me and Bernadette get home safe, and help me and the other law-enforcement guys catch the guy who's after her. I pray You'll stay in the middle of our thoughts and our feelings so that we always know Your mind and obey Your will. I pray in Jesus' name. Amen." He pressed her hand gently. It was her turn.

Still overwhelmed at his unexpected maturity and at the intimacy of going with him into God's presence—even on a smelly, noisy public bus—she could hardly speak. "Thank You for Your protection so far," she finally managed to get out. "Thank You for teaching us to trust You. Please help me to learn Your mercy, and help me not to be afraid…." Her throat closed. "Amen," she whispered.

Owen nudged her shoulder. "Why don't you try to get some sleep now? It'll make the trip go faster."

"How long until we get to Reynosa?"

"About three more hours. Here, lay your head on my shoulder."

She didn't even try to argue. "Okay."

Making herself comfortable, she closed her eyes again and let her thoughts drift. Peculiar to feel so safe. Protected. Loved.

Paul Grenville had been dwelling on Briggs's last phone call all day. The more he thought about it, the more convinced he became that he needed to take a stronger role in the situation.

Which was what brought him to the Shelby County Public Library on a beautiful spring Saturday afternoon, when normally he'd be cleaning the gas grill on his patio, getting ready for his daughter's family to arrive for their weekly barbecue. He always played Horse with his two grandsons while the burgers cooked and the ice-cream freezer did its thing in the kitchen sink.

Grenville had worked hard, made many sacrifices in order to enjoy these private family times. Certainly, he had been somewhat selfish and stupid in his younger days and had come close to paying the price with his marriage. But he'd recovered by carefully covering his tracks, eliminating everybody who might tarnish his reputation.

Well, almost everybody. There were still two left: Bernadette and Ladonna.

He found a computer at an unoccupied table in the nonfiction stacks. Few people patronized this area of the library. And those who did wouldn't know him, as this was a branch nearly twenty miles from his home in Germantown, east Memphis—and his face hadn't yet started making the national news. The Web sites he pulled up would be nobody's business but his.

A quick Internet search brought up nothing on *Ber-*

nadette McBride—not surprising, since he'd tried it at least twice. But typing in *Bernadette Malone* fetched a short article in the *Fort Worth Star-Telegram* about seminary students serving on various mission fields. He studied it for a while, fascinated by the idea of the little hooker who'd gotten away from Ladonna all those years ago—reformed enough to become a missionary.

The mind positively boggled.

It hadn't been easy to locate her on the Yucatán. He'd had to rely on a couple of trusted sources, Briggs being one of them. Generally speaking, Briggs was dependable. That he had let the girl get away in three different locations made Grenville wonder if his faithful employee was being paid by somebody else.

He shook his head. Briggs knew if he ever turned on Grenville, he'd be dead within twenty-four hours.

The girl had gotten away by sheer luck. She was smart, but Grenville was smarter. For example, he knew that the pilot's father had been killed in a shoot-out nearly three years ago and posthumously disgraced because of involvement in smuggling drugs and illegal aliens.

He held this information in his hand like a particularly strong suit of cards. Royal flush, baby. Royal flush.

Ten kilometers outside of Reynosa, Owen decided to awaken Bernadette. He'd been watching her sleep, nose buried in his shirtsleeve. Understandable—three or four different brands of obnoxious cologne had given him a nagging headache.

Now he had to think about how to proceed once they got inside the States. No way was he going to let Bernadette go to Memphis—or anyplace else, for that matter—on her own. She didn't have to tell him a thing, but he was going to follow her around until he found out on his own. And, mercy notwithstanding, he was going to use every investigative tool in his power to put the guy after her behind bars.

"Benny." He touched her cheek and watched her eyes open. She sat up and blinked, scrubbing her hand over her mouth.

"Huh? Where are we?"

He smiled. His shoulder seam had pressed a neat curved crease across her forehead, just like a rainbow. "We're coming into Reynosa. It's gonna be tricky getting you in without your ID, so I want you to let me do the talking when we get to the Border Patrol checkpoint. Okay?"

"Sure. Have I been asleep this whole time?"

"Like a baby. Want to know what you said in your sleep?"

Her eyes widened. "I don't talk in my sleep!"

"No." He traced his finger along the rainbow on her forehead. "Unfortunately you don't. And you don't snore, either. I was just kiddin'."

She reached down for the backpack and took out his comb. Unplaiting her hair, she hid her face.

He folded his arms and watched. "I would have called Eli by now, but I forgot to get the phone from you and didn't want to wake you up. Did you ever get hold of Meg?"

"Oh, sorry." She dropped the comb and dug in her jeans pocket for the phone. "No, you yanked me out of Noé's truck before I could call her. Then we started running and I forgot to try again. Here." She handed it over and busied herself with the comb again.

He glanced out the window, then opened the phone and searched through the phone numbers. Reynosa was a growing industrial city known for its *maquiladoras*, or bonded assembly plants. All kinds of American electronics corporations had concerns here. Labor was cheap, dependable and close to the border. Reynosa was also a major crossing point for illegal immigrants. He was going to have to do some fancy tap dancing to get Benny across.

Eli answered on the first ring. "Where are you?" said his brother without preamble.

"Fixin' to get off a bus in Reynosa. Is there any way you can come get us? Benny's documentation is a little sketchy."

"You should have called before now. I'm nearly four hours away." Eli paused. "I'll make some calls to the McAllen station and see if I can get you permission to bring her across. I'll get there as fast as I can."

"Thanks. Listen—" Owen hesitated, glancing at Benny. "What did you find out from the Torreses?"

"Not much. They're just as dumbfounded as we are that somebody's taken to shooting at our girl. I guess you're gonna have to get it out of her. But Jack did say that he'll pull whatever strings he needs to for her protection. She should come straight to the police when she gets across the border, report what happened and let them handle it."

"Okay. If I can get her to listen to reason." Intercepting Benny's sudden frown, he grinned. "She's an independent lady."

"Well, we're talking felonies here. Attempted murder is no joke. She'll have to get over the independence."

"You want to tell *her* that?"

"No. I'll let you handle it." Owen could hear the smile in his brother's voice. "Look, you two get off the bus and lay low somewhere until I can get you straightened out with immigration. I'll call you back when I get on the road."

"Thanks, Eli." Owen closed the phone and braced himself.

Bernadette bent to tuck the comb into the backpack. "I'm not going to the police."

"Why not? You're an American. People can't shoot at you and get away with it, even in a foreign country."

"It's my word against his. I'm not subjecting myself to an investigation."

"Wait a minute!" He stared at her in disbelief. "I was right there and I saw him aim at you and shoot. Two different times. I can't identify him, but *you* can."

"Didn't you hear me? I have other people's reputations to protect besides mine."

"Reputations? Benny, we're talking about your *life!*"

"And yours." She pressed the heels of her hands against her eyes. "That's what makes this so hard."

"So what do you propose to do, since you object to the smart thing?"

"What I intended to do all along. Go to my friend in Memphis."

Owen tried to remember what she'd said about this person in Memphis—if anything. She? He? One of the old boyfriends? One of the men who had known Benny before she was his?

His? In three days she had gone from a woman he was attracted to and intrigued and challenged by to the other half of himself.

Mine. Maybe in this case it was okay to be selfish.

"All right, then. I'm coming with you."

"Owen…" she groaned, sliding her hands across the top of her head.

"If you can be stubborn, so can I. Just try leaving me behind."

ELEVEN

The Border Patrol station in McAllen, Texas, was nothing to write home about, in terms of amenities for civilian visitors. But coming home from a long stay in a developing nation, Benny felt as if she'd just moved into the Waldorf-Astoria.

While Owen made phone calls and filled out reports, she made herself at home in the break room. She had access to a coffeepot, a wide selection of abandoned mugs and a small television set with a fifteen-inch screen. Filling a mug that said I Left My Heart in San Francisco with surprisingly fresh coffee, she settled on a metal folding chair to watch the late news.

It seemed like a hundred years since she'd caught up on the American political scene. She flipped through the channels, trying to find a report that wasn't vulgar, violent or antireligious. The ho-hum nature of infidelity, drug addiction and insider trading seemed a little freakish when she'd just returned from a place where the very basics—food, water and shelter—defined everyday life.

She was just about to turn the set off when a familiar face on a cable news program caught her attention.

"—here in the White House, where sources say the President has begun to compile a short list of nominees for the recently vacated attorney general Cabinet post.

"One of the top names for the position is Tennessee Supreme Court Chief Justice Paul Grenville. Grenville is a moderate judge with Southern roots and a tough record for dealing with drug traffickers. Having been friends with this extremely popular president since their law-school days, he is likely to sail through Senate hearings toward confirmation this summer...."

Benny's weary body and overloaded brain would hold no more information. Numbly, she pressed the power button on the TV remote. Grenville's hateful face blinked off.

She wished she could just as easily erase her memory.

"Miss Malone, would you like another cup of coffee?" The deferential young agent who had been assigned to keep Benny company poked his head into the break room for the third time in an hour.

She shook her head. "Haven't finished this one yet. But thanks."

Agent Kevin Padilla rapped his knuckles on the door frame and grinned. "Okay, ma'am, but you just let me know if I can do anything to make you more comfortable. Carmichael says—"

Padilla abruptly disappeared and Owen leaned in the doorway. "Carmichael says we can go now. Eli finally got you cleared."

Benny stood up, deliberately blanking out the images uploaded into her brain by the news report. "Oh, I'm so relieved."

"Eli will be here in just over an hour. He's gonna take us to San Antonio. We can spend the night there with him and Isabel."

"That would be wonderful." A real bed with clean sheets. *Thank You, Lord.* She owed a lot to Owen, too. He had to be worn out, but he'd taken care of her first. "I think everything's squared away with my job. I called my supervisor and the substitute can stay one more week. That'll give me time to…"

Time to blow up everything she'd built over the last thirteen years? No wonder Ladonna had insisted she come to Memphis. Had she known Grenville had aspirations to this powerful office?

The White House Cabinet.

If he went through those kinds of hearings, every person who had ever known him would be interviewed. If some reporter, or even some political rival, ever dug up her old name, she would be dragged through the mud again—this time on the national news.

Grenville had to know this, too. That was why he had killed Celine, Tamika and Daisy—her three companions from Ladonna's house—and why he'd sent that hit man to the Yucatán.

She took a breath. "I'll have time to replace all those clothes I left behind in Agrexco."

Briggs's cell phone rang as he waited in line to go through the American checkpoint on the Reynosa-Hidalgo-McAllen International Bridge. He plugged in his earpiece and thumbed the talk button. "Yeah, boss."

"Briggs, where are you?"

"Just about to go through customs on the bridge. I

told you I missed them in Reynosa because of that flat tire—"

"Yeah, yeah. I know. Look, there's been a change of plans. Since you didn't get her in Mexico, where it would have been a whole lot easier—"

Grenville paused, and Briggs started to apologize again.

But the judge didn't give him a chance. "Now we've waited too long. Did you see the news tonight?"

"When have I had a chance to watch the news?" Briggs tried not to sound too sarcastic. The judge expected a certain amount of respect.

"I suppose you're right. Anyway, some enterprising print reporter dug up the president's list and stuck it in *The Commercial Appeal* up here. The wire services will have it by morning, and it may even be on the evening news tonight. If we don't get to this girl fast, she's going to realize what kind of power she has."

Briggs felt lead settle in his gut. In so many words, the judge had just given him an ultimatum. "Boss, I've been trying—"

"I know you have. I know you, and you've never let me down yet. Which makes me think somebody may have warned the girl before you got there."

"Warned her? Like who?"

"I don't know. That's what you've got to find out."

"But don't you want me to keep after her?"

"Yes, but first I want you to head for that orphanage in Acuña before she gets there. Dig through her files, her computer, whatever you can, and see if you can turn up anything useful."

"But boss… I'm right behind her and Carmichael now. I could take them out easy—"

"Think, Briggs. They're on the run, no telling where right now. Even if you found them, it's too risky to blast away with a gun in an American city. We've got to be smart. Plan ahead."

"You think I'll be able to find her again?"

"Whatever you find in her computer will lead you straight to her. I'm sure of it. Go on across the border, get a good night's rest and catch the first flight to Del Rio in the morning. Rent a car there and head for Acuña."

Briggs had hoped not to see Mexico again unless it was a resort vacation. He sighed. "Okay, boss. I'm on it."

When it was his turn at the checkpoint, he flashed his badge and got out of the car. Two courteous port-of-entry agents inspected both of his disassembled guns, which he had stored in the trunk of the Crown Victoria.

"Are you about finished here?" He injected just a trace of impatience into his voice.

"Yes, sir. You're good to go. Have a nice evening."

He planned to. Cruising into McAllen, Texas, the City of Palms, he decided to sample the nightlife before retiring to a hotel. Yes, he was going to have a *very* nice evening.

Eli hooked his elbow across the back of the seat. "Y'all want something to eat before we get on the road to San'tone?"

Owen, in the front passenger seat of Eli's Border Patrol SUV with Bernadette directly behind him, wished he could treat everybody to a steak dinner. Under the circumstances, not a good idea. He loved his brother, well, like a brother, but here he was, back to feeling like one of John Wayne's sidekicks.

"Anything but burritos." Owen turned to wink at Bernadette and she smiled.

"I'm thinking Chinese."

Just in case the hit man had caught up to them, they'd left by the back door, with Eli going first to make sure the coast was clear. It was galling to be so out of control in the situation. A target.

At least the SUV's tinted windows should hide Bernadette's identity. He wished they could scare up a couple of U.S. marshals to guard her, but she wouldn't accept that much protection. Owen supposed he should be grateful she allowed him and Eli near her.

"Okay, Chinese drive-through it is." Eli turned around and started the car.

Thirty minutes later, they were on their way north, teasing Eli for refusing to handle chopsticks and drive, the SUV filled with the exotic odors of kung pao chicken and stir-fried vegetables. By now it was nearly eleven and Highway 281 was fairly deserted.

Owen finished his own meal and half of Bernadette's, then stuffed the trash in the take-out sack. He didn't have to wait long for Eli's questions.

His brother cut off the radio. "Okay, you two, spill it. What's going on?"

Owen watched Bernadette's shoulders tense. He hated that she'd had so little emotional respite, but Eli had to know how to help them. Much as he didn't want to admit it, she was likely to drop something to Eli that she hadn't told him yet. He held his peace.

"Come on, Benny," Eli said gently. "You know I'll help however I can, and anything you say to me is confidential."

"Eli, I know that." Bernadette laid her head back against the seat. "It's not that I don't trust you."

Owen ruthlessly suppressed a surge of some foreign emotion. Hurt, maybe? *This is your brother, man. Let him help.*

But he couldn't help remembering the night last summer when Benny had called Eli, hysterical over the sudden death—murder, as it turned out—of one of her orphanage kids. Dulce Garcia, smothered by her pillow because she happened to look very similar to a young murder witness—a witness who had become Eli's adopted daughter.

And Owen had never asked her why she'd called Eli instead of him. He couldn't without sounding like a jealous chump. And he was *not* jealous of his happily married brother.

Still, he waited, breath held, to see how she'd answer. If she blurted everything out to Eli after refusing for the last three days to tell Owen anything, he'd—he'd—

Well, what *would* he do? Suck it up and be a man, that's what. Do everything in his power to keep her safe.

"Okay, then, if you trust me, you've got to give me some idea who we're up against." Eli glanced at Owen. "I understand if there are things in your past you'd rather not share. But we can't help you if we're boxing at shadows."

Half a mile rolled past before Bernadette sighed. "That's true. But like I told Owen, my past is all mixed up with somebody else that I have to protect. She has a family, a new life, and she's in as much danger as I am."

"What could be more dangerous than someone trying to kill you?" Owen asked incredulously.

"I know what you're thinking, but I'm all alone. No family, no ties to anybody else. I promised this woman I'd keep her secret for her family's sake."

Owen wanted to kiss some sense into her. "You've got more ties than anybody I know! There are people who love you and depend on you, and I'm not going to let you throw yourself under the bus like this!"

There was a shocked silence. An eighteen-wheeler roared past with a gust of wind. Then Eli let out a breath. "Okay, calm down, Owen. Nobody's throwing anybody under a bus." He paused. "Benny, what do you want us to do?"

She dabbed her fingers under her eyes and Owen felt like a jerk. "Just help me get to Memphis with as little hassle as possible. I don't mind if Owen comes, but nobody else. Please."

Suddenly, Owen's world turned right side up. She wanted him and nobody else. Not in a romantic way, but still…. Maybe she wasn't angry with him for pressuring her for three straight days.

There was just one little problem he had to iron out.

Bernadette stumbled into Isabel Valenzuela Carmichael's outstretched arms and had to fight the urge to burst into tears.

Pulling back to see her friend's face, she found the feminine compassion she'd had no idea she needed so desperately. Even at three o'clock in the morning, sans makeup and dressed in a chenille bathrobe, Isabel looked like a Latina movie star.

She also looked wide awake and highly maternal. "Come sit down for a minute." She clasped Benny's hand and drew her toward a homey family room featuring a stone fireplace, a huge leather recliner and two big sofas on either side of a glass coffee table. Gently pushing Benny onto a sofa, she turned to Owen. "Go on in the kitchen—I made cinnamon buns for breakfast, but you can have one now. I want to talk to Benny."

"Okay, I know when I'm being booted out." Owen shrugged and disappeared into the kitchen with Eli. "Cinnamon buns." Benny heard his voice drift back. "You lead such a hard life, man."

Isabel's dark eyes twinkled. "Owen's always hungry, no matter how much you feed him. How about you? I can run and get you one, too."

"No, thanks. We ate Chinese on the way up here." She reached for a sofa pillow and tucked it against her side. "I apologize for getting you up in the middle of the night. I told Eli we should just come in quietly and sleep on the couch."

"Are you crazy?" Isabel blinked. "When I haven't seen you since Christmas? Were you able to sleep in the car at all?"

"Some." Benny yawned. "Owen's just like that battery-operated bunny. He just keeps going and going. But I'm dead."

"I imagine. We moved Mercedes in with Danilo for the night so you can have her room, but I thought you might want to wind down for a few minutes first."

"Yes, but if you don't mind, I'm too tired to answer questions. Can we just talk about kids and sewing and college classes?"

Isabel's shrewd look said she understood Benny's reluctance to get into the details of her adventure. But she smiled. "I never mind talking about my kids. Danilo's taking the first grade by storm. Literally." Isabel shook her head. "Just yesterday, his class was practicing for their spring musical. On the way out of the auditorium, he unplugged the custodian's vacuum cleaner. Shut down maintenance for a solid two hours before they could figure out what the problem was."

Bernadette laughed. "He was only being a clown."

"Eli says he's just like Owen, and he's driving me crazy!" But Isabel chuckled, too. "Mercedes, on the other hand, is doing so well in her speech classes we can't believe it. She still signs, of course, but she loves to practice talking, and her English lipreading is amazing."

"Bilingual lipreading. That's a wonderful gift." Though profoundly deaf, Mercedes had been largely responsible for the apprehension of the man who had killed Dulce and kidnapped Isabel and Danilo last year. Benny couldn't wait to see the little girl and give her a huge hug. "Is she still drawing?"

"We signed her up for after-school art lessons at the university. In the morning, I'll show you some of her most recent work—oops, I guess that's in just a few hours."

"What is today, anyway?" Benny suppressed a yawn. "I've completely lost track of time."

"Saturday. I'm so glad I have a day to spend with you and Owen without worrying about classes. Eli's off duty until Monday, too."

"I'm afraid I've put him in a bad spot, but I'm so grateful he could come get me and Owen."

"Eli lives to take care of people. And so does Owen."

The curious look in Isabel's eyes was inevitable. Bernadette turned her head. They were friends, but not on as intimate a level as she'd been with Meg. "He's been very good to me."

"Of course he has. He's been in love with you for over a year. Why do you think he took that mission supply-drop assignment?"

"Because he's a good guy and he loves to share. It didn't have anything to do with me." She hoped. She felt that ridiculous wave of heat creep up her neck again. Oh, she was too tired and distraught to deal with this.

"Benny, I know when a man is ready to settle down. I've been through this twice myself, remember?" Isabel's first husband, also a Border Patrol agent and Jack Torres's partner, had been killed in the border incident involving Eli and Owen's father. She'd been happily married to Rico Valenzuela for five years.

Benny looked over her shoulder to make sure their voices hadn't carried into the kitchen. She heard the men laughing over something Owen had just said. "Well… well, maybe he's ready, but I'm not."

"Why not? Benny, he's a strong Christian, he's got a great job and goodness knows, he's a doll! What are you looking for?"

"I'm not looking for anything." Why was that so hard for people to understand?

"Maybe he's been coming on a little too strong. I can't imagine anybody being intimidated by Owen, but is that it?"

Benny pressed the heel of her hand to her forehead. "Oh, for goodness' sake, no! Isabel, can't Owen and I just be friends?"

"I'm not sure." Isabel looked troubled. "I'm positive he…but maybe I'm wrong." She gave herself a little shake. "But listen to me, pestering you when you've just come home from such a hard trip, when you're probably dying to go straight to bed. I'm sorry. Come on, if you're sure you don't want something to eat or drink, I'll show you where the bathroom and Mercedes's room are."

Benny followed Isabel into the kitchen, where Eli and Owen sat at the table, sharing a plate of gooey cinnamon rolls and a carton of milk.

"Eli!" Isabel huffed. "I thought we agreed you weren't going to drink out of the carton anymore."

Eli looked guilty. "Owen made me do it."

"I did not! You said you didn't know whether the dishwasher had been run."

"Never mind." Isabel sighed. "I wanted you to know I put a pillow and some sheets in the coat closet for Owen. Can you help him make up the couch while I get Benny settled upstairs?"

"Sure." Eli picked up the plate of pastry. "I'll just put these away first."

"I don't know why he'd bother," muttered Isabel to Benny. "They ate all but two of them. I'll have to start all over for breakfast."

Benny smiled as she followed Isabel up the stairs.

Owen wandered into the family room and found the linens Isabel had left for him in the closet. He didn't see his brother more than once or twice a month now that Eli had married and moved away from the border so that Isabel could go to college. Still, he was almost as comfortable in their home as he was in his own apartment.

They always offered to move six-year-old Danilo out of his bed for Owen, but he preferred to sleep on the sofa. He liked to get up early, raid the refrigerator and take a glass of orange juice out to the back deck to read the paper. Once the kids got up, he'd play "Uncle Owen," bouncing on the trampoline with them, swinging Danilo on the tire swing, taking a cup of pretend tea with Mercedes. She was such a *girl,* and he enjoyed teasing her with exaggerated bad manners.

Eli, apparently having dealt with the remnants of the cinnamon rolls, came out of the kitchen to help him set up the roll-out couch.

"Sorry if I got you in trouble." Owen flipped open Isabel's crisp sheet. He held it to his face and sniffed. She liked to hang things in the fresh air and they always smelled so nice.

"She wasn't mad. Just teasing you."

"How could you tell? She looked mad to me."

Eli got that goofy "Isabel" look on his face. "I'm getting to where I know her really well."

"After eight months? You still got a lot to learn, boy."

"Maybe so. But I'm happy."

Owen snorted. Well, duh. He stuffed the sheet under the bottom of the mattress with less than military precision.

Eli fixed it. "So what's going on with you and Benny? She reminds me of that cat Mom used to have. Remember when you blasted it with your Super Soaker?"

"Only you would bring up my youthful indiscretions at a time like this. I did not squirt Benny with a water cannon."

"That's not what I'm saying!" Eli scowled. "I'm just saying she looks really nervous around you. What have you done?"

"I haven't done anything!" He glanced toward the stairs. He could hear the shower running, but lowered his voice anyway. Isabel didn't need to know what a neurotic mess he'd turned into. "You'd look a tad traumatized, too, if you'd been shot at and chased halfway across Mexico."

"Yeah, yeah." Eli plopped into the recliner as if it wasn't nearly four o'clock in the morning. "All that aside, I thought you went down there to sort of stake your claim with her. Get her to come home."

"I never said that!"

"Owen." Eli shook his head. "This is me, remember? The guy who taught you how to drive? Your chauffeur for your first date? Does she *know* what you went down there for?"

Owen gave up on defensive pride. He sat down on the sofa bed and bent to take off his shoes. "I think so," he muttered toward his feet. "We kind of talked around it."

"So what did she say?"

"I never realized what a nosy Nelly you are." He sighed and flopped backward onto the couch. "Remember when we were up in my chopper, looking for the guy who killed Dulce?"

"Yeah, why?"

"You told me that day that going after Benny was a hopeless case." He swallowed hard. "Well, you were right."

"I was an idiot. Don't pay any attention to that man behind the curtain."

"Ha. You're dealing with the Cowardly Lion here, man. I'm about ready to give up on her. I mean, how many different ways can a woman say no?"

Eli looked skeptical.

"Okay, listen." Owen decided to shoot straight. He needed his brother's counsel. "I do love her. You know I do. But she's not exactly what I thought she was. What you said a minute ago struck home with me—about getting to know Isabel over the last eight months." Eli's eyes widened and Owen backtracked. "I don't mean Bernadette and I got, uh, intimate or anything like that. I just mean we've been together a lot. Through thick and thin, as they say. It changes the way you think about a person."

Eli frowned. "Maybe you'd better explain a little more."

"Well, for example. Every time I touch her, she flinches. Not like she's afraid of me, but more like—" he fumbled for words "—like she's afraid of herself. You watch her. She's affectionate with Isabel and the children. She even hugs you freely. But let me get within a couple of feet and boom, she freezes up. She relaxed a little bit toward the end of the trip, when we had more important things to think about, like staying alive. But, Eli, I can't marry a woman who won't let me touch her!"

He looked away, the outburst having come from somewhere in his gut that he didn't even know was there. Eli opened his mouth to reply, but Owen held up a hand to forestall him and sat up, restless.

"Man, that sounded beyond selfish." He put his head in his hands. "I know there's a reason for it. Somebody hurt her a long time ago and it had nothing to do with me. I just don't know if I'm strong enough to deal with it."

Eli lowered the recliner footstool and leaned forward, elbows on knees. "Listen, brother, don't sell yourself short," he said quietly. "If anybody can love her past whatever the problem is, you can. Or, rather, the Lord *in* you can. Don't imagine that Isabel and I have this perfect understanding all the time. She's got issues with losing Rico like she did that we're *still* getting over. It just takes time. Lots of prayer. Communication. Strong counsel."

Owen looked up and met his brother's gaze. The compassion there made his eyes burn.

Eli smiled. "I'll leave you alone and let you get some sleep. Just know that Isabel and I are praying for you, and you can talk to me about it anytime. Okay?"

"I hear you." Sighing, Owen dropped onto the pillow. "Just do your best to keep Danilo from jumping on me at the crack of dawn."

TWELVE

Briggs had had enough airport experience lately to last him the rest of his life. As it turned out, he got little actual R & R at the hotel. But despite a crashing hangover, he was up at the crack of dawn to make his seven-o'clock flight out of McAllen-Miller International Airport. Nobody could say he wasn't diligent about fulfilling his responsibilities to the judge.

In one of those stupid flukes of the airline industry, he had to take a short hop northeast to Houston in order to fly west to Del Rio and probably wouldn't get across the border to Acuña until late afternoon.

Somehow, he didn't care. Just get him in a semivertical position and he'd be out like a light.

After going through security and checking in at the gate, he found a booth in the café and ordered a plate of pancakes while he read the newspaper. Might as well find out what was going on in the world. As the judge had predicted, the list of nominees for attorney general was on the front page of the national section.

Whoo-ee. The fat was about to hit the fire. Grenville had better get ready for some good old-fashioned Washington, D.C., mudslinging. Other than this Malone girl, he shouldn't have any problem. Thanks in large part to Briggs himself, the man's reputation was clean as a whistle.

Briggs would just have to make sure it stayed that way. Bound to be a hefty reward when Grenville got established in Washington.

Acapulco, here I come.

Benny woke up with something breathing on her cheek. Brushing at it, she rolled over and came in contact with a cold, wet nose attached to an ugly brown half Labrador, half something else.

The Carmichaels' dog, Fonzie.

He gave a happy *woof* and licked her chin.

"Hey, Fonz," she croaked, "who let you in?"

A glance at the open door answered that question. Danilo, dressed in shorts, T-shirt and black cape, beamed at her. "Aunt Benny! You came to see me!"

"I sure did." She shoved her hair out of her eyes. "Come give me a hug."

He barreled into the room, dove across the dog and landed on the bed.

Benny held him tight, though she wasn't sure if she was participating in a hug or a wrestling match. "Where's your mommy?"

"In the kitchen. She's making Daddy and me stay out of the dough, and Owen's outside having his prayer time, so I decided to see if you was up."

"I'm glad you did. Did you bring Mercedes with you?"

"Yep. But she's out in the hall. I don't know why she wouldn't come in."

"Go get her and tell her I need another hug."

Danilo dashed for the door and came back holding his eight-year-old sister by the hand.

Mercedes was adopted, but it was startling how much the children favored one another. Both had the warm brown skin tone, big dark eyes and thick black hair of Hispanic descent, but the similarity was more in a bright, intelligent, well-loved expression than physical appearance.

Benny held out her arms, beckoning with her fingers. Mercedes's face lit. She dove toward Benny with nearly as much enthusiasm as Danilo. Pulling back, the little girl enunciated carefully, "I'm glad you're here."

Teary-eyed at the deaf child's enormous progress since the last time she'd seen her, Benny cupped her sweet little face. "I am, too. I missed you." She drew her feet up cross-legged to make room for the children. "Thank you for letting me sleep in your bed."

"Where have you been?" Danilo bounced into the middle of the bed as if it were a trampoline, while Mercedes sat in ladylike fashion on the edge.

Benny hauled Danilo into her lap before he could make another leap. "In Mexico. Helping the doctors and dentists."

Danilo's eyes widened. "I *like* my dentist! He gives me bubble gum toothpaste and tickles my teeth. See? My front one is getting loose."

Benny obligingly wiggled the little tooth offered for her inspection and whistled in admiration. "Won't be long."

"Mercedes gets a whole quarter under her pillow when she loses hers. I'm gonna buy a comic book when mine falls out."

Mercedes laid a gentle hand on Benny's arm to get her attention. "I drew you a picture."

"Did you?" Benny smiled. "Then let me get dressed and we'll go look at it. Maybe the cinnamon rolls will be ready by then."

"Okay." Mercedes slid off the bed.

But Danilo latched on to Benny's neck. "I wanted to tell you about my comic book!"

Mercedes intervened, vehemently signing something to Danilo.

Looking chagrined, he signed something back.

Mercedes repeated her motions and Danilo reluctantly released Benny. "Oh, okay. I'll tell you about it later." He ran for the door. "But hurry!" he shouted as he slammed it behind him.

Shaking her head, Mercedes lifted her hands as if she were eighteen instead of eight. "Boys," she said clearly, then followed her brother, towing Fonzie by the collar.

Benny took a quick shower in Isabel's upstairs bathroom, luxuriating in warm, parasite-free water. The tub was clean but crowded with plastic action figures and fat wax tub crayons. She washed her hair with Sponge-Bob SquarePants shampoo and smiled as she dried off with a Disney character beach towel. Made her look forward to getting back to Acuña to see her kids.

She couldn't help wondering which of them would still be there by the time she made it back. Sometimes extended families insisted on bringing the children home, and on rare occasions, foster or permanent homes turned up. The teenagers, sadly, sometimes moved out to pursue deplorable jobs in the area's bars and brothels.

Those were the ones that broke her heart.

But she had to make a decision about what she was going to do about Grenville. She knew who he was, what he had done—to her and to other young girls like her. For all she knew, he still preyed on teenagers. The thought brought nausea rolling into her stomach.

She stood at the bathroom mirror, wrapped in the robe Isabel had loaned her, hands flat on the counter. Did it show? Could anybody tell what had happened to her?

Unclean, whispered the ugly voice that trapped her sometimes when she least expected it. *Not fit for His love.*

Not fit for anybody's love.

Fists clenched, she battled it. Eyes open. Truth.

Truth, Bernadette.

Out loud, she repeated words that had sustained her for years. "But when the kindness and love of God, our Savior, appeared, He saved us, not because of righteous things we had done but because of His mercy. He saved us through the washing of rebirth and renewal by the Holy Spirit, whom He poured out on us generously through Jesus Christ, our Savior."

Crying, she relaxed her shaking hands and looked in the mirror. Clean outside, new inside.

Owen sat on the back patio with his brother, a glass of iced tea at his elbow. With half an ear tuned for Bernadette's voice, he scratched the dog behind his floppy brown ears. For the last fifteen minutes he'd been watching the kids tussle on the trampoline like a couple of puppies. Danilo kept double-bouncing, upsetting Mercedes's graceful gymnastics. One day she was going to whop him upside the head and it would all be over with.

He wished Benny would hurry up and come outside to keep him company. He'd never particularly noticed Eli and Isabel cooing like a couple of domestic pigeons—or if he did, it hadn't bothered him. But Eli had just now snagged his wife around the waist as she walked by with a plate of fresh cinnamon rolls and pulled her into his lap.

"Eli, at least let me put these on the table," she protested, as he kissed her under her ear.

"I'll take 'em," Eli said.

Owen looked away, uncomfortable, but he couldn't block out the sound of Isabel's soft giggle.

"Excuse me, guys." He got up and headed for the sliding glass door. "I need to make a phone call."

"But you haven't eaten—" Isabel gasped, as Eli chuckled. "Quit, Eli!"

"I had half a dozen of those things in the middle of the night, remember?" Owen went into the house and yanked his cell phone out of his pocket. Oh, brother. If he ever got married, he'd be more considerate of innocent bystanders.

He dropped into the recliner and speed-dialed the station in Del Rio. One of the guys on duty answered. Sounded like Kennedy.

"Hey, this is Carmichael. Is Dean there?"

"Carmichael! You back? How was old Mexico?"

Everybody down there knew everybody else's business. But he wasn't about to fill a kid like Kennedy in on the particulars. "Not too bad. Can I speak to Dean?"

"Yeah, sure. Just a sec."

Owen waited, glancing toward the stairs. Hold off for just a few minutes, Bernadette.

"Dean here. What's up, Carmichael? You through messin' around with the señoritas across the border? Ready to come back to work?"

"Well, that's just it, sir. I'm hoping you'll approve another week's leave for me."

"Another *week?* Why?"

"Something came up while I was down there. My plane had a problem and I, well, I had to make an emergency landing in a barn."

"And…"

"And I've got to, uh, take care of the problem. I had to leave the plane there, so… It's just not a good situation, sir. I'd like to straighten out the mess before I come back to the sector."

"Carmichael." Dean hissed out his patented irritated sigh. "This sounds like something I really don't want to know. Is this…problem…something you can take care of in three days? Say by Wednesday?"

Owen mentally calculated. The earliest he could charter a plane to fly Bernadette to Memphis would be Monday. Two days' travel, plus whatever time it took her to take care of her business…

"I don't think so, sir. I really need the whole week." Owen had never been one for groveling. He gritted his teeth. For Bernadette. "Please, I'll work night shifts for the rest of the quarter."

"You may be doing that anyway," growled Dean. "We're shorthanded because recruiting's down with everything that's been in the news lately." He paused and Owen waited. *Please, Lord.* "All right, Carmichael, but this is *it.* Get your keister back here by a week Monday."

"Yes, sir. I will. And thank you."

Owen hung up before Dean could change his mind.

He heard a footfall on the stairs and looked up. Bernadette stood on the bottom step, a hand on the banister. She had on one of Isabel's yellow sundresses with a pair of sparkly flip-flops. Her hair was damp and flyaway, and her eyes were huge.

"You're going to fly me to Memphis?"

"Gotta find my Daisy Jane," he joked, quoting an old America song he liked.

She walked toward him. "I can go by myself."

"We've already covered that territory. You said I could go with you. No takebacks."

"I didn't think you'd be able to get off work."

Hurt seared him. He stood up. "The only reason you said you wanted me was because you didn't think I *could?*"

"That's not what I—ooh." She crossed her arms in front of her stomach. "Don't be such a baby, Owen. Of course I want you to come. I just don't want you to get in trouble with your supervisor. I know he can be kind of a bear."

"Okay, sorry." He ran a hand around the back of his neck. "Well, he said I could go. But I can't get hold of a plane until Monday. So I have a plan if it's okay with you."

"Monday? But I wanted to leave today."

"I know, but there are a couple of reasons why we shouldn't." He walked toward her, just so he could get a closer whiff of that vanilla stuff. She smelled like a cookie. "First of all, if the hit man's still looking for you, he'll be watching the airport today and tomorrow. If we wait until Monday, we may stand a better chance of sneaking out. Also, I thought you might like to go to the Riverwalk this afternoon and do a little shopping. We both need clothes, right? We can blend into the crowds, get something to eat, listen to the music…"

He stepped closer, but something in her expression warned him to stop. He saw goose bumps on her arms, and the tender spot under her jaw worked.

She wanted to say yes, but she was going to say no anyway. She opened her mouth.

"Okay, we'll do it," she said in a rush, as if she were outrunning herself. "But just as friends, okay? This is not a date, right?"

"Right." He sighed. "I wouldn't dream of making a date with you."

Hearing Owen beg for another week off did something to Benny's resistance. But maybe she could handle an evening in his company without coming unglued. Or letting him lure her into dropping her guard.

She stood in front of Isabel's closet, trying to choose an outfit that would make her feel in control of the situation. "Owen said it would be warm this afternoon and chilly tonight." She looked over her shoulder.

Isabel stood behind her, hands on hips, a thoughtful frown puckering her fine black eyebrows. "That's true. Springtime here can be unpredictable. I think you should just wear the dress you have on and bring my denim jacket to put on when the sun goes down."

"Okay, but what about shoes? I don't think the flip-flops will work for much walking. I could put my sandals back on—"

"No, no, no!" Isabel looked horrified. "Don't you dare spoil that pretty dress with leather huaraches. I made it to go with these flip-flops. Just wear them and when you get to town you can buy some new flats."

Benny sighed. "There's just one problem. Everybody wants me to shop for clothes and shoes, but I don't have any money. And I don't get paid until the end of the month." She winced. "Missionaries don't make much money."

Isabel smiled. "I consider this my own personal mission project. Owen will buy what you want, then I'll pay him back. If you had time, I'd sew for you, but this is an emergency."

"Isabel, you and Eli don't exactly have money running out your ears, either! You're in college, and with the two kids—"

"I'm on a full scholarship," Isabel said with justifiable pride. "My mother helps out with child care when we need it, and Eli just got a raise. So there." Her full lips quirked.

"Okay. One outfit, then. But don't let Owen talk you into letting him pay for it! That just wouldn't be—wouldn't be right."

"Deal." Isabel pulled a feminine little denim jacket out of the closet and handed it to her. "But don't forget to buy underwear," she added with a twinkle.

Trust Isabel to be practical. "That's going to be interesting, with Owen hanging around. Maybe I can send him to look at knives or something." Benny smiled. "I have one more favor, if you're still feeling charitable. I need to borrow your computer and send an e-mail to the Garretts before Owen and I leave for the Riverwalk.

They're the missionary family I was helping down in Agrexco. I'm sure they're wondering what in the world happened to me."

"Of course. I should've thought of that. Come on, the computer's in my sewing room. You can have some privacy there."

A few minutes later, Benny was seated at the computer, trying to remember the Garretts' e-mail address. It wasn't easy to compose a simple explanation for her disappearance that would make sense. In the end, she simply wrote, There was an emergency and I had to leave with Owen. I'm sorry to have left you in the lurch like that. Please forgive me. We're safely back in the States and I'll e-mail again when I get a chance. If you could mail my phone to me, I'd appreciate it. Take care. Love, Benny.

Well, that's short and sweet, she thought, pulling up her Internet service provider's Web site. Just cut to the chase and leave out anything that tells what really happened. *Oh, well, I'll make it up to them later.*

Owen parked Eli's truck at the Alamo's visitors' lot and got out to help Bernadette down. He liked the fact that she waited for him to come around and open her door. Like Isabel, she was a perfect lady.

Both women were petite, dark-haired and dark-eyed, too. But the resemblance ended there. Isabel had the ivory skin tone of a classic Latina, with a rounded figure and quick, decisive motions. She tended to be chatty, too, and laughed easily.

Bernadette, on the other hand, reminded him of pre-Civil War photographs he'd seen of beautiful French Quarter quadroons. Slight, languid, reticent. Mysterious.

She lightly gripped his fingers as she slipped to the ground but immediately let go. "Thanks." She stepped around him, clutching her jacket.

"Have you ever been through the Alamo?" he asked as they picked their way down the uneven sidewalk. It ran along a busy street, and Saturday traffic was crazy, even midafternoon.

"Sure. I've brought groups of kids here before. It's one of my favorite historic places." She looked at him. "Kind of sad, though. All those people who died."

"Lots of heroes in the story, though. Davy Crockett, Jim Bowie—Eli's the history nut in our family, but Dad made us come a couple of times when we were growing up."

"I take it that wasn't your idea of a good time."

"Well, like you said, it was a bit solemn for me. I preferred the camping trips."

They walked past the ancient outer walls of the Alamo mission onto the Plaza. Pigeons strutted on the sidewalk, families picnicked on the shaded benches and some guy was standing on a box preaching fire and brimstone to anybody within shouting distance. A few yards away, a cotton-candy stand sprouted fluffy pink and blue treats.

"Want one?"

Benny shook her head, her gaze on the preacher. "Wonder if anybody ever listens to him."

Owen shrugged. Wild-eyed fanatics like that made him squirm. Which was weird, because Benny was a missionary, too. She made him squirm in a completely different way. Amused at the thought, he caught her hand. "Come on, let's go across to the Riverwalk." When she gave him a look, he smiled. "I don't want to go off and leave you."

They crossed the street and walked a few blocks to the outdoor stairs leading down to the entrance of the Hyatt Regency. The Paseo del Alamo—the Alamo passage through the hotel—was a beautiful walk in itself. Owen couldn't have cared less about the waterfalls, colorful mosaic tiles and shop windows, but he enjoyed Benny's admiration. She stopped once to run her fingers over the tiles, as if trying to absorb the imagination of the artists.

Inside the Riverwalk itself, they walked along the shaded sidewalk without talking. The afternoon was bright and not too hot, with relatively low humidity, given the proximity to the water. They had to dodge afternoon shoppers, though not nearly as many as Owen had experienced during summer tourist seasons. The water flowed calm and brown, with the occasional tour boat drifting by.

Bernadette seemed withdrawn, though she allowed him to keep hold of her hand. She glanced at people eating at the sidewalk cantinas and restaurants and watched shoppers going in and out of the stores, smiling only at the children skipping along with parents or grandparents. He couldn't quite interpret her expression. Pensive, maybe.

He finally bumped her shoulder gently with his arm. "What are you thinking about?"

She blinked and looked up at him. "It's just so…odd, being in this hedonistic tourist trap. You know, after all we saw and went through last week. I guess I'm having a little bit of culture shock."

"I can understand that. But I'm not going to feel guilty for being an American. For having a good job, making money and being able to spend it on what I like." He squeezed her hand. "And right now, I like spending it on you. I want to buy you something." He gestured grandly at an array of shops to their right. "How about some ice cream or something?"

"I think I'd rather save my appetite for supper— some barbecue, maybe." She wrinkled her nose. "But before I forget, I'll tell you what I do need. We have to split up for a few minutes. Isabel gave me some money to buy a few personal items. Is there someplace I can find things fairly inexpensive?"

"Your wish is my command, ma'am. There's a little dollar store down at the end of Houston Street, I think. Let's go."

THIRTEEN

While Bernadette was in the dollar store, Owen wandered down the walkway by himself. Hands in the pockets of the jeans he'd borrowed from Eli, he peered into shop windows without much interest. If he and Benny were going to buy clothes, the mall would have been a better choice. But he'd wanted to give her a relaxing afternoon.

Shopping wasn't his idea of relaxation.

Maybe he'd take her on one of those riverboat tours, even though they'd both heard all the San Antonio history so many times they could probably spout it with the tour guide. Then he'd buy her dinner in an outdoor restaurant, where they could hear the mariachi bands from the Mexican cantinas.

He saw an empty bench under a stand of fan-leaf palms and thought about sitting down. The sound of running water surrounded him, and lush greenery and flowers filled every nook and cranny. The parks commission went to a lot of trouble to keep the place clean. Even the pigeons were well behaved.

Too restless to sit, he crossed an arched stone bridge to check out a knife store on the other side of the river.

Bernadette wanted him to meet her back at the dollar store in an hour, so he had plenty of time to kill.

He'd been buying knives as souvenirs since he was a kid and had quite a collection back in Del Rio. This shop had a decent selection—the bone-handled switchblade was pretty nice, but it was also priced for tourists. He knew of a little hole on Durango Street where he could pick up the same thing for about half the price.

Keeping his wallet in his pocket, he went back outside and walked on. This wasn't nearly as much fun without Bernadette. Eli always told him the class clown needed an audience. Well, maybe so, but he couldn't help it. She'd been gone for fifteen minutes and he was already lonesome.

Three doors down, a jewelry store caught his eye.

He'd never voluntarily been inside one, though his mom occasionally dragged him and Eli with her when they were on vacation. Without knowing why, he made a beeline for the glass-fronted shop. He propped his hands flat against the window and stared at glamorous displays of rings, bracelets and necklaces on blue velvet. Gold and silver and platinum settings, filled with stones of every description.

His gaze immediately latched on to a simple smoky topaz ring, emerald cut, set in gold. Not too big, not too small—just really elegant—it sat on an island to itself, as if disdainful of the bling surrounding it.

Wouldn't that look great on Bernadette's small, long-fingered hand?

Like she would ever let him give her a ring. He could just hear her now. *Owen, what would people think if I let you start giving me things?*

They'd think we were engaged. A real couple.

The idea had built in slow stages for so long he couldn't have pinpointed when it started. Now that it was in his head, he couldn't get it out.

He was going to ask her to marry him. Not now, when her attention was on dealing with whatever drew her to Memphis. Not until they caught the shooter.

But one day soon. What if he bought her a ring now and saved it for the right time?

Eli would tell him to wait. Be patient. Let her pick out her engagement ring. But come to think of it, Eli had picked out Isabel's ring and she hadn't objected one bit.

Pushing open the jewelry store's front door, he walked into cool air-conditioning, quiet music, deep carpet. *I'm gonna drop some money in here.*

Overtime is your friend.

"Hi, can I help you?" An elegant woman put down a watchband she'd been polishing and approached him from across the counter.

"I'm just looking at rings," he blurted. Where had his famous easygoing charm flown off to? His heart was racing like a cutting horse. He took a calming breath.

She smiled. "For you or for a lady?"

"A lady. A young lady I'm thinking about…" His hand went around the back of his neck.

Her eyes lit. "An engagement ring?"

"Yeah." Now that he'd said it out loud, confidence took over. "I'm just beginning to look around. She doesn't know yet." Boy, that was the understatement of the year.

"All right. Did you just want to look, or do you want me to show you something specific?"

"How about that smoky topaz in the front window? I like that."

"Topaz for an engagement ring? That's kind of unusual."

"Would it be wrong?" What did he know about rings?

"No, not wrong. Just different." She walked to the window, unlocked the case and brought out the velvet display tray holding the topaz ring. "Diamond solitaires are traditional, but this is a personal thing. You know what she'd like best." Back at the counter, she slipped the ring off its little blue velvet finger and handed it to Owen. "What's your lady's name? Tell me about her."

Boy, this woman was good. He was ready to buy this ring already. "Her name's Bernadette. She's small, kinda dark-skinned. Long, curly black hair and black eyes. She's a very brainy woman."

"Brainy, huh?" The clerk gave Owen an embarrassing once-over. He was glad he'd worn a cap to cover the streaky hair. "Obviously she is if she's got you looking at engagement rings." She laughed when Owen squirmed. "Sorry, couldn't resist. Would you like to look at some diamonds, too? Just to compare?"

"No, I really like this one." He flattened his palm and held it up to catch the light. He might be impulsive, but he knew he had good taste. He hadn't had any trouble deciding on Bernadette.

Besides, his hour was nearly up.

"I'll take it." He pulled out his wallet.

If the woman thought he was a certified mental patient, she hid it well. She took the ring from him, found a velvet-lined box and began the process of setting Owen back a couple months' pay.

"I want some earrings for her, too." He couldn't give her the ring for a while, and he wanted something to give her tonight after dinner.

The clerk looked up from the computer cash register and blinked. "Sure. Pierced?"

"I don't know." He closed his eyes, trying to picture Bernadette's dainty ears. "Yeah, I think so. In fact, I think she's got two in each ear."

"Okay, then, look at these. It's kind of a new thing." She opened another case and showed him a stand of long, gold spirals that connected with each other on thin, delicate chains. "They're called threaders."

"Hey, that's cool. I'll take two pairs of those—one's for my mom." He cleared his throat. "Can you wrap them separate from the ring?"

"Absolutely." She winked. "Bernadette is a very fortunate young lady."

Recklessly, he plunked his credit card onto the counter. "I hope she'll think so."

Owen's behavior had been very peculiar all afternoon. Ever since she'd met him outside the dollar store, he blushed every time she looked at him. Then he would tug on the bill of his cap, look away and ask her if she was hungry. Or thirsty. Or too hot or tired of carrying her packages.

Finally, just to shut him up, she let him buy her an ice-cream cone. They sat on a metal bench under a tree, a little way down from a big Mexican restaurant where a mariachi band, playing on the front steps, entertained passersby. A slight breeze blew fragrant odors from the restaurant, along with the sounds of the trumpets and guitars. Peppers, corn, cilantro and a hint of the bougainvillea blooming in pots near the bench.

She ate her ice cream, relaxing.

Then Owen stretched his arm along the back of the bench.

Get over yourself, she told herself, glancing at his hand dangling near her shoulder. *Let him be himself.*

And Owen was affectionate. He was a wonderful uncle to Eli and Isabel's children, answering Danilo's endless questions and admiring Mercedes's drawings as if they ought to hang in the Louvre.

"You keep looking over your shoulder," he said. "Mr. Hit Man couldn't have followed us here."

"I'm sure you're right." Let him think she was nervous about that. She certainly hadn't forgotten it, though she felt safe enough for now.

"Let's take inventory. You got what you needed at the dollar store?"

She nodded, blushing. She'd had just enough money for a few intimate garments, some toiletries and makeup. "I'll have to see about a trip to the Salvation Army thrift store when we get to Memphis, though. Now I know how people feel when they have a fire or flood." She gave him a rueful look. "I didn't realize how attached to my belongings I was."

"I'm amazed how well you've gotten along without them. My mother would be going into a decline."

"I've met your mother and she's not that shallow. She's a beautiful lady who loves to give. I know she's been personally supporting a couple of my orphans."

"Yeah, she's all right. She's beginning to get over my

dad." Owen scratched his nose. "I think she's even got a boyfriend. How weird is that?"

"Not weird at all. Sounds perfectly normal to me. It's been, what, two years since he died?"

He nodded. "About that. Seriously, I'd be glad to see her find a good man who'd keep her company. With Eli stationed over here now and me working so much…" He withdrew his arm from behind her shoulders and reached into his pocket. "Hey, I want to show you something I got for her. See what you think."

Delayne Carmichael wasn't the only one in her family who loved to give. Owen opened a small white box. Inside it lay a pair of fine earrings, long twists of gold unlike anything she'd ever seen.

"Ooh. Pretty…." She took out one of the earrings and let the central chain dangle across her index finger. It glinted in the late afternoon sun. "She'll love these."

"You like them? They're not too gaudy or anything?"

She looked up at him. His brow was puckered, anxious. "Gaudy? Oh, no. They're really elegant. She can wear them with anything—jeans all the way to eveningwear." She held the golden spirals up to her own ear. "See?"

His eyes crinkled in a smile as he stared at her. But he wasn't looking at the earrings. Something flared under her rib cage, something dangerous and as wild as the eagle he reminded her of.

When had this happened? When had she turned the corner from friendship and mild infatuation toward a growing spiritual admiration and love?

"I'm glad you like them," he said, "because those are yours. I bought Mom some, too, but hers are silver and they're still in my pocket."

"They're...mine?" All the breath left her body. "Owen, you can't—"

"Yes, I can. I told you, I spend my money on what I like, and that means you. Come on, Isabel bought you those jeans and shirt and shoes. Can't I buy you a pair of earrings?"

She carefully laid the earring back in the box with its mate. The box jiggled in her shaking hand.

Owen placed his palm under hers, steadying it. "You don't have to tell anybody where they came from," he said gently. "You'll just know I gave them to you because I love you."

Her gaze flashed to his. His blue-green eyes were so tender, his heart offered to her openly. She wanted to cast herself into his arms, even in this public place. "I have to tell you something," she whispered.

"Not now. Put on the earrings and let's go have dinner."

"We just ate ice cream." She gave a watery chuckle.

"Then let's go on a boat ride and then have dinner."

"Owen..."

He covered the earring box with his other hand, cupping hers between his. "I'm getting tired of arguing with you, lady. Will you please put them on?"

She closed her eyes to hide from his emotion. "Okay."

It took three tries to get the delicate gold spirals threaded properly in her earlobes, and she had to ask Owen to carry the studs she'd been wearing in his pocket.

Finally, he surveyed her with obvious satisfaction. "You're beautiful," he said simply and took her hand to tug her to her feet. "I saw the boat-tour ticket booth across from the Hilton. Let's go stand in line."

Oh, dear Father, she prayed silently as they waited

their turn for a boat. *How did this happen? Why? You know I'm committed to serve the Mexican people. He loves me, he said! It's not fair to him, because I have to tell him what I've done and it'll change everything.*

Sickening fear knotted her stomach, more painful than the terror of stopping a bullet. She'd known rejection before. But not from the man she loved.

She remembered the day she'd met Miranda Gonzales, a godly young woman who'd reached out to a brokenhearted teenage call girl. She'd been sitting on the toilet in a Peabody Hotel restroom, sobbing her eyes out because one of her lovers had decided to go back to his wife. That had turned out to be the best day of her life.

You don't have to tell him. Let him think you were just a giddy college student and had a few boyfriends before you knew the Lord.

Meg had advised her a long time ago that she didn't have to reveal anything she didn't want to about her past. She'd read somewhere that sharing too many details gave glory to the adversary and wasn't a necessary part of confession.

That was true to a point. But when her past affected her relationship with a potential life mate…

She couldn't forget Owen's face when she'd told him she'd been promiscuous. Shock. Momentary distaste, though he'd quickly recovered.

Oh, dear God, why did that happen to me? Why did I let it happen?

At six o'clock that evening, Briggs hit the entry point from Del Rio, Texas, going into Acuña, Coahuila, Mexico. The difference between Reynosa and Acuña was stark.

Driving a Dodge Rendezvous through the little old town, he found poverty butted up against old money like a bum sleeping next to one of the Hilton heiresses. The middle of town wasn't so bad, though the roads could use some improvement. But the farther he got out of town, the deeper the slums.

He simply could not understand Americans who volunteered to live in poverty like this. Tiny cinderblock homes, many of them roofless, defined a patchwork stitched together with plywood, tar paper and cardboard. Most doorways and windows were uncovered, glass almost nonexistent. A thin procession of light poles lined the main highway, with a frightening number of wires extending from each pole out into the sprawling colonies.

One good streak of lightning and the whole place would go up in flames.

Once he turned off the paved road, he was in a tenement of sorts, at least fifty years back in time. Gimpy vehicles were parked along the rutted dirt roads, with an occasional yellow school bus—obviously somebody's home-sweet-home—sitting off in a weedy patch of rocks.

Twice he stopped to ask directions—*"¿Orfanato?"*—and both times wound up more lost than before. Eventually he came across a young man, coming home from a day at one of the American factories on this side of the Rio Grande, who spoke enough English to get him where he was going.

Four or five twisting turns up a knotted hill and there it was: Niños de Cristos Orphanage. Two neat, white-washed one-story buildings with tin roofs and cracked sidewalks. Off to one side a play yard with children climbing all over a swing set, a slide and monkey bars. Somebody had cared for this place.

He stopped near the front door, where a couple of little girls sat reading, and got out of the car. *"¡Hola!"* Smiling his charming smile, he approached the children. They looked up at him with interest but no fear. "English?"

One of the girls shook her head, but the other said, "Yes, sir. *Un poco.*" She gave him a gap-toothed grin. "Nicho and Faye in the kitchen." Jerking her thumb toward the second, longer building, she went back to her book.

Nicho and Faye were the substitute houseparents, an American husband-and-wife team sitting in while the Malone woman was off on her hurricane-relief endeavor. Briggs had discovered this while pretending over the phone to be the pastor of a church interested in financially supporting the orphanage.

He could go find the houseparents, make up some story about why he needed to search Bernadette's room. Or he could go in quickly, get the job done and leave without them any the wiser.

He chose the latter course.

This building was clearly the dormitory, and the windows all seemed to be wide open. *Good enough.* Briggs headed to the rear of the building, ostensibly toward the cafeteria/common room. But as soon as he was out of sight of the two little girls, he veered behind the dorm.

As expected, there was a back door, but it was locked. These people were too stupid. He leaned inside an open window right beside the door and turned the dead bolt. In a matter of seconds he was inside.

Judging by the size and layout of the building, it looked like a two-room dorm—one side for girls, the

other for boys. Four sets of bunk beds lined the walls of
this room, with simple wooden shelves providing space
for the children's meager belongings. Through an open
doorway at the end, he could see a shower and toilet;
there was a closed door leading, he hoped, into the
houseparents' room.

He found this door locked, but breaking in was a
simple matter of running a credit card between the door
and the jamb. *Stupid, people. Really stupid.*

Entering the closetlike little room, he found evidence
of the Malone woman's occupation, as well as that of
the current houseparents. A weird little pen-and-ink
drawing—a skinny guy in glasses and a fishing hat with
a lizard on it—hung over the queen-size bed. Drawings
autographed to "Aunt Benny" were tacked with push-
pins on a corkboard over the desk. Several plastic flower
leis adorned the bedposts. A PC sat on a desk under the
window.

Bingo. He sat down in the desk chair and booted up
the computer.

Within ten minutes, he had hacked in. He pulled up
the e-mail program and scanned through the most recent
received messages. Nothing struck him until he went
back nearly six months and found an e-mail from
somebody named Ladonna Sherman.

Hi, Bernadette,
Thank you for writing to check on me again. You'll
never know how much your forgiveness and compassion mean to me. I'm doing well, but the doctor still
watches me like a hawk. I think he's afraid I'll go back
to using. It's only the grace of God that I don't. I'd

love to see you if you ever get back to the Memphis area. I know you'd never tell another soul where I am. I count on your discretion. Anyway, I understand that hearing from me is probably painful, so I won't bother you again. Please know that I pray for you daily and count you one of the dearest blessings of a good and faithful God.

In Christ, Ladonna.

Briggs turned on the printer, printed the e-mail and got out. He'd found what he was looking for.

FOURTEEN

By the time they boarded the boat, dusk had fallen. Lights had blinked on all over the Riverwalk—in the trees, inside the shops and restaurants, along the bridges.

It looked like a fairyland scene from a Disney movie.

But a chill had dropped over the river with the setting of the sun, and Benny slipped on the jacket Isabel had sent with her. She moved a little closer to Owen in an effort to absorb his warmth.

They sat near the back of the boat, where the breeze was less intense. A group of teenage girls occupied the seat in front of them, their squeals and giggles echoing with childish joy. The tour guide, who identified himself as a local college student hungry for tips, kept up a running commentary that Benny and Owen mostly ignored.

She had a hard time concentrating on anything but him. Over the last few years, she'd built, carefully, one block at a time, a reputation for diligence, responsibility, integrity.

Wisdom.

Here and now, she felt like one of those airheaded teens—happy as she had never been in her whole life.

She'd been full of joy in the Lord. Grateful for His rescue. Secure in the knowledge that, whatever happened in her life, she was bound for Heaven and she was loved in the most intimate way possible by her Creator.

But this…

This giddy, heart-stopping knowledge that Owen cared for her…

She wanted to do something completely uncharacteristic. Stand up and rock the boat. Jump up and down and wave her hands. Twirl like a ballerina.

Crazy.

He bent his head to murmur in her ear. "What are you smiling at?"

She shivered, unable to look at him without breaking out in a grin. "Nothing. I'm just happy."

"Are you warm enough?" He tugged her closer, wrapping his arm around her shoulders so that his hand cupped her elbow. She was tucked against his chest.

Scandalous, and she didn't care. After all, they were in public, with people everywhere.

She reached up to touch one of the earrings dangling against her neck. "I'm perfect."

"You are."

At that, she looked up. "That's not what I—"

The look in his eyes stopped her. His gaze dropped to her mouth and the eagle took flight in her chest again.

"Listen to me, Bernadette." He lowered his head so that only she could hear him. "I don't know what happened to you before I knew you. Don't think I don't care, because everything about you matters to me. But there's plenty of time for you to tell me who hurt you and why and all that." He stopped for a moment, lips pressed together.

She started to answer, but he shook his head.

"No, listen. I want to say this. You've got to know how much I want to kiss you. You're a very bright woman—" he laughed softly "—and I'm an out-in-the-open kind of guy. But I'll never pressure you. In fact, I'll wait until you offer to kiss me. As long as I have to, I'll wait for you."

Tears burned in her eyes. "Owen, it's not what you think—"

"I don't care what it is. And I really don't want to mess up our day together. I just want you to know I love you. I've loved you since the day we took the children to the river last summer."

Did he think she was afraid of him? She had never wanted anything more desperately than to fall into the love he offered, to drown herself in it and pretend she deserved it.

Not fair that she had nothing to give Owen but a broken spirit and a remorseful heart. Since she'd known him, she'd done nothing but take from him.

A kiss was all he wanted right now. The only thing he'd ever asked of her.

She was scared to death she'd mess that up, too.

Shuddering, she reached up and laid her hand against his cheek. "Come here." She pulled his head down just enough that her lips met his and clung for a stinging moment of sweetness. And then his mouth opened a little, inviting her to stay. Yes, she thought, and found herself pulled under, lost in Owen's goodness and the way he loved her. No one had ever kissed her like this, intent on healing her, making her feel cherished and beautiful.

When he stopped and laid kisses on the bridge of her nose and under her eyes, she realized she was crying.

"Was it that bad?" He sounded amused.

"I'm a mess." She hid her face in his shoulder.

"That's okay. I'm a slob, so we'll make a great couple."

"Owen, we can't—"

"Sorry, folks, it's my bedtime so I've got to boot you out. This is my last tour of the night."

Startled, Bernadette jerked and bumped heads with Owen.

He gave their young captain a mock scowl. "Your timing stinks, man." He sighed. But he stood, gave Benny a hand and helped her step off onto the pier. They stood in a puddle of light under an old-fashioned street lamp as the tour guide tied the boat down. "I guess we have to go back to Eli's. Want to go to church in the morning?"

"Of course." She tried to regain her equilibrium, though her unsteadiness came from emotion rather than the gentle sway of the boat on the river.

She needed a time of concentrated praise and worship and Scripture study more than she'd ever needed it in her life.

Owen had no idea what the preacher said in his sermon. He had passed the morning in a fog of bliss interrupted only when Isabel towed him into the computer room after breakfast and demanded the receipts from Bernadette's clothes so she could write him a check. He told her to go pester Eli for a while, then asked her if he could borrow a Bible.

He automatically stood up with the congregation when the invitation hymn was played. Bernadette had kissed him. Voluntarily, sweetly and thoroughly. Or maybe it had been the other way around and he had kissed her.

They had kissed each other, and he loved her so much, he wanted to haul her off to a justice of the peace *right now* before she could change her mind.

Isabel, perfectly aware of where Benny's new earrings had come from, had warned him not to be stupid. "You can borrow my Bible," she'd said, "but don't rush your fences."

"That's an English riding term, not Western," he'd informed her and wandered back into the kitchen for another biscuit.

Okay, he thought as he followed Bernadette and the rest of the Carmichael clan out of the church building toward the family van. So I sit on it for a while. She's certainly not going to give herself to anybody else. We go to Memphis, take care of whatever business she has there and come home to Del Rio. I can wait.

He repeated it to himself. *I can wait.*

"Coldwater, Mississippi? You mean all this time, she's been right here under my nose, twenty miles away?"

Grenville was pulling out of the church parking lot, trying to get across town before everyone beat him to Morrison's. He always took the entire family, grandkids and all, out to eat every Sunday. Marjorie used to cook a pot roast with rice and gravy, but nowadays, the clan had gotten so big, he liked to give her a break. They could afford it.

She had no idea who he was talking to or what it was about. Didn't care, either. In fact, she was on her own cell phone, trying to calm their daughter Kristin down. Kristin was always mad at her husband, Joey, these days. Poor guy worked sixty hours a week and still couldn't do anything right.

"Are you sure that's the right address?" he demanded.

Briggs let out an irritated sigh. "I checked and re-checked. It's got to be the same woman. The dates are right, social security number, everything. I would've told you last night if you'd had your phone turned on."

"We were at the opera. You don't turn on your cell phone when you're in the Orpheum. Very bad manners." Grenville glanced at Marjorie, who had just closed her phone and stuck it in her purse. "Listen, just get up here and take care of the problem. I have to go to Washington tomorrow morning for preliminary hearings. I want the issue settled by the end of the week."

"You're with the wife, aren't you?" guessed Briggs.

"Yes, and the stakes are enormous."

"Okay, boss, I'm on it. But you need to put some more money in my account. I'm running low on cash."

"Money's no problem. Don't call me again until you have the situation under control."

Briggs mumbled something unintelligible, then cut the connection.

Grenville removed his phone earpiece and smiled at his wife. "Are they still meeting us at the restaurant, honey?"

"Yes. She's just tired from being up all night with the baby." She pulled down the visor mirror to check her lipstick. "Didn't Bob and Teresa Denton move down to Coldwater a couple of years ago?"

"I don't remember."

How much had she heard?

"I'm not sure I want to go up in a plane with you again." Benny hung back as Owen finished the exterior part of the preflight inspection. He'd called in a favor from a friend in order to borrow this single-engine Cessna Skyhawk to take her to Memphis. At least, that was what he'd told her.

What kind of friends did he have, rich enough to *loan* him a plane? It wasn't a cargo plane like the one he'd flown down to Mexico—the one they'd left in Gustavo's barn, which somebody would eventually have to retrieve. This was a single-engine plane, albeit a very cushy one with leather seats and gleaming instrument panel. And they were going all the way to Memphis in it.

Unless she changed her mind.

He looked around after examining the propeller, a broad grin on his sunburned face. "What's the matter, lady? Got butterflies?" This morning he'd washed his hair so many times, the cheap black dye had turned to a streaky dirt color. Wearing Eli's brown leather bomber jacket, he looked like a rock star.

Did she have butterflies?

"Yeah, the size of a pterodactyl. That last experience kind of took my breath away."

"Hey, lightning never strikes twice in the same place. Besides, how else are you gonna get where you want to go?"

"I'm partial to the bus, myself."

"That would take twice as long. You said you were in a hurry."

She sighed. "I am. That's the *only* reason I'm going to put on a blindfold, plug my ears and get in that cockpit with you."

"You know why they call it a cockpit, don't you?"

"No, but I'm sure you're going to tell me."

"It started with the fighter pilots of World War I. That's what we are, Benny. A team of fighter pilots."

"Owen, why are you doing this? You don't have to go."

With one step he was right in front of her, tall and compelling. Fearless.

"You know why. Any time you need me, Bernadette, I'll be there. In fact—" he grinned "—I'll be there whether you want me or not. Now come on, let's roll. Time's a-wastin'."

Owen's college frat brother, Johnny Stapp, happened to be a licensed pilot as well as an FBI agent. Currently stationed in San Antonio, Johnny had been glad to arrange for the plane, the fuel and hangar space in Memphis. The only stipulation was that he be included in the wedding party when Owen finally got around to proposing.

Which Owen assured him would happen at the earliest opportunity. Just as soon as he could get up the nerve.

He figured he'd at least made a step in the right direction with the earrings and the kiss. Twice he'd told her he loved her and she hadn't said it back. But the look in her eyes said more than words.

After an uneventful four-hour flight, they were taxiing up to a tie-down space at Wilson Air Center at Memphis International Airport. The third leg of their adventure had begun. Not that he was complaining. Owen liked adventure as much as the next man. It was just that he *really* preferred to know where he was headed.

A couple of avionics techs ran to help him park and tie down, so professionally and smoothly that the process took less than fifteen minutes. Owen helped Bernadette down from the plane and kept a protective hand at her back as they crossed the tarmac to the terminal.

She looked casual but put together in the clothes she'd bought in San Antonio—slim jeans, a pink long-sleeved knit top and white leather shoes with girly flowers across the toes. The concierge, a young man in a Wilson Air polo shirt, gave her an appreciative glance as he showed them to the pilots' lounge.

"Make yourselves at home, sir, ma'am," he said, smiling at Bernadette. "Agent Stapp left instructions to provide you with whatever you need in the way of business supplies. We have computers, fax, printer… and we have a snack bar if you're hungry or thirsty." He stopped in the doorway on the way out. "Let me know if I can assist you in any way."

"I think you've made a conquest." Owen stretched his weary back. Johnny's plane was comfortably appointed, but it had been a long flight from San Antonio.

Bernadette wandered over to the window, which looked out on the busy airfield. Owen walked up behind her, hoping she'd turn around and offer a kiss. She'd been quiet all morning and he didn't know how to reach the place they'd been Saturday night.

"What's on your mind, Bernadette?"

Her shoulders lifted. "Trying to figure out how to tell you about Ladonna Sherman and—and Berna-dette McBride."

"Who?" He laid his hands on her shoulders. The bones there were as small and fragile as a sparrow's, the muscles tight. His stomach started to hurt. "Is Ladonna the one who sent you that e-mail? The one that started all this?"

"Yes." She turned to look up at him, expression sober.

"I'm sorry I didn't give you the whole story from the beginning. But I hoped I wouldn't have to involve you. And then when we crashed and it took so long to get here… By the time I realized you *were* involved, I couldn't figure out how to…" Her lips were trembling and she lifted her fingers to cover them. "Owen, I'm so sorry."

He didn't have the heart to make her feel any worse than she already did. If only he knew what was at the root of her troubles.

"Okay, don't worry about it. You're talking now. That's the important thing."

She looked at the closed door of the lounge. "Are you sure nobody will come in on us?"

"Can't guarantee it. You want to go somewhere more private?"

Her eyes widened. "No! I mean…this is fine. But can we sit down?"

"Sure." He led the way to a conversation area with a leather sofa, a television and a couple of wing chairs. He chose the sofa, hoping Benny would sit beside him. She edged onto one of the chairs. Distance.

Oh, man. Not good.

What to do with his hands? He placed them on his thighs.

Bernadette twisted her fingers. Finally, he cleared his throat. "Did you want me to just ask you questions?"

"No, I—I'll just start from the beginning." A tiny flash of humor lit her eyes. "The very best place to start, according to Maria in *The Sound of Music*."

He smiled. "Okay, so you were born…"

"Let's not go *that* far back." She sighed. "I already told you I was a foster kid. The usual scenario. Unwed mother trying to raise me alone, boyfriend after boy-friend…" She swallowed. "One of them molested me."

He tensed. Maybe he'd known it deep down. But still, when she said it out loud, he wanted to hit a wall with his fist. Or the guy who had done that to her. No, what he *really* wanted to do was hold her. But she sat apart from him, stiff as a mannequin in a store window.

"I'm sorry, Bernadette." He didn't know what else to say.

"Yeah, me, too." She looked at her fingers. "After that, I didn't really care anymore what happened to me. Just wanted to be happy. And I couldn't get happy there with my mama, so I ran away. Several times until—until the state *took* me away from her."

"Was that when you met Mrs. Coker?"

"Yes. She lived not too far from here." She looked out the window, as if Mrs. Coker might be standing out on the tarmac. Owen wished he could kiss the blessed woman's feet for being kind to Bernadette. To his sur-prise, Benny laughed softly. "I told you she gave me a Bible. After that, I sort of had a Bible fetish. I stole them from every foster home and hotel room I stayed in. Kept them under my bed."

"Hotel room? Why would you be in hotel rooms?"

The blood drained out of her face, then came back with a rush to her cheekbones. She actually shrank into her chair. "The last time I ran away, I wound up on Beale Street in Memphis. I was always crazy about Elvis and it sounded so romantic to be there, where he recorded. I went into the lobby of the Peabody Hotel to watch the ducks and got to talking to this man."

There was something peculiar in her voice, a deadness

he'd never heard before. Owen jerked to his feet. "Stop. I don't need to hear any more. Just skip to where this Sherman lady comes in." He was being a coward, but he couldn't listen to what he knew was coming.

"This is it. This is how I met her." She looked up at him and the blind pain there sent him to his knees in front of her.

"All right, then. Go ahead, just…" He shook his head. "Bernadette, I don't know how to deal with this."

"Well," she said reasonably, "you asked for it. You wanted me to trust you, and this is who I am. I told you you wouldn't like it."

"Yeah, you did." He covered her hands, knotted in her lap, with his. "Only, would you please come sit with me so I can touch you?"

"No, because it's important that I see your face."

"Then I'll stay right here." Dread crashed around in his chest. "Go ahead."

She took a sharp breath. "That man took me to a place down near the other end of Beale, where other girls my age lived. With a woman they called Sister Zena. She was sort of a mystic, into palm readings and mojo bags and voodoo dolls and all that creepy nonsense. Her deal with us was that she'd let us live there if we'd give her part of what we made." She paused. "Owen, you're hurting my hands."

He loosened his grip immediately, brought her hand to his lips and kissed it. "I'm sorry," he said helplessly. *Oh, Lord. Lord, what do I do?*

She sighed. "She was awful, and I was afraid of her, but none of us could leave. We didn't have anyplace else to go."

"How old were you then?"

"Fourteen."

"What does a fourteen-year-old do to earn a living on Beale Street?"

She blinked at him. "Owen, don't you understand? I sold myself. I was a prostitute."

FIFTEEN

She saw it register on that open, all-American-boy face when her words sank in.

"You were a…" He physically flinched, as if he'd been punched in the stomach. "No."

In a detached sort of way, she was amazed that she had no tears. Maybe she'd cried them all out a long time ago. She felt a little sorry for Owen. "You know it's true. I sure wouldn't make something like that up. It's almost like it happened to somebody else, it was so long ago and I've come such a long way. I lived there on Beale Street for about nine months before Miranda came."

Owen shook his head again. He seemed to be having a hard time processing her words. No wonder. "Miranda?"

"Miranda Gonzales. The Lord Jesus sent her to Memphis on vacation that summer. We met in the Peabody Hotel restroom. She heard me crying after I got stood up one day and followed me to Zena's house. I would never have gotten out without her."

"That's a mighty wild story."

"You can see why I don't tell it. It's complicated and makes people uncomfortable." She searched Owen's eyes. He was more than uncomfortable. He looked flayed alive. A tinge of anger crept through her chest. *I'm the one who was abused and betrayed.*

"You're okay now, right? The people who brought you out of there…they took care of you?"

She felt his big hands gripping hers, saw the anxiety in those turquoise eyes. A stronger wave of pity for him filled her.

He wanted everything tied up neatly like a romance novel. He wanted a perfect sweetheart who came to Christ and never had another impure thought.

Well, she couldn't give him that woman. All she had was herself, broken and pieced back together. She could feel herself withdrawing.

"Not right away." She sighed, straightening a little. "I went back to the children's home in Collierville, but it wasn't a perfect place, either. At least I was back in school. Finally, after about a year, the Gonzaleses got custody and took me in."

"And that's where you became a Christian." Some of the color returned to his face.

"Yes."

He stayed on his knees in front of her, looking down at his thumb rubbing across her knuckles. "So how does all this relate to the guy who tried to kill you? And how does the Sherman woman play into it?"

"Ladonna Sherman is—*was* Zena."

"You became friends with your madam?" His mouth hung open.

"Is that so impossible? I changed. So did she. Owen, Christ is powerful. The Holy Spirit can work miracles in people's lives."

"Yeah, but—"

"Look, it's not like we're best friends. A few years after I left, a local church was doing renovations on the river end of Beale Street as a mission project. Somebody got brave enough to tackle Ladonna's house and told her about the Lord. After she became a believer, she changed her name, left town and started a new life."

"What made you get in touch with her?"

"I didn't. It was the other way around. She found out where I was and called one day. To apologize. To try to make it up to me." She squeezed Owen's fingers. "Which was ridiculous, and we both knew it, but eventually I forgave her. We've kept in touch off and on, once or twice a year. I changed my name, too, by the way— to Malone. It used to be McBride. And I started calling myself Benny."

He stared at her for a moment, soaking that in. "So where is Ladonna now?"

"In Coldwater, Mississippi. Just south of the state line, about twenty miles from here."

"Is that where we're going?"

She nodded. "She doesn't know I'm coming. I wanted to make sure I could actually get here before I called her."

"Okay." Owen frowned. "That explains a lot, but I still don't understand what she has to do with the hit man. And your three dead friends. Was that a lie or—"

She snatched her hands away and reared back. "I don't lie! Especially not to you!"

"Wait!" He reached for her. "I didn't mean—"

"I know I've dumped a lot on you. You can wait for me here while I go to see Ladonna—"

"Bernadette, don't treat me like that." He sat back on his heels, seeming to realize she wasn't going to let him touch her again. "I just want to understand what's going on."

"All right, I'm sorry." She pushed her fingers into her hair. "The three women used to be in Ladonna's house when I was there. We were pretty close friends. Ladonna wrote to me when Daisy died of an overdose five years ago. It didn't even make the news. Then a couple years later, Tamika was found strangled, with no clues as to who did it or why. Ladonna e-mailed me the night before you and I left Agrexco. Celine's body had washed up on the riverbank, cause of death unknown."

The stark, bare facts still horrified Bernadette. Three young women linked to her and to Ladonna. Murdered?

Owen echoed her thoughts. "You think they were all killed by the same guy and now he's after the two of you?"

"I wouldn't have assumed so, but that guy showing up at the clinic and asking me if I knew Daisy—less than twenty-four hours after I heard from Ladonna... As far as I knew, *nobody* knew who I was in my old life, except the Gonzaleses, of course. And Meg and Jack Torres. And nobody but my close friends know who I work for and where I've been for the last three months. So for the FBI to show up like that, well, it made me nervous.

"So that morning I had the Jeep sitting ready to go, close to the dorm. Just intuition, I guess. Then he shot at me." She shuddered. "And here we are."

"But, Bernadette, we should have gone straight to the police. Even the Mexican police would have protected you. I know a few cops down there—"

"No. You don't understand who this guy is. He's got

tentacles everywhere. Remember, he found us, even after we crashed in the middle of nowhere. I had to get up here to talk to Ladonna and decide what to do. Right now, it's just my word against his. I have no proof of anything."

"*He. This guy.* Who are you talking about, Benny?"

"Judge Paul Grenville. The man who first took me to Ladonna's house."

"Grenville?" Dazed, Owen shook his head. "You mean the guy the President wants to appoint as Attorney General?"

"Yes."

"The hearings start this week. Today."

"I know. That's why I've got to get to Ladonna today."

He felt like some blockhead who couldn't comprehend a simple sentence. "A Tennessee Supreme Court judge solicited teenage prostitutes—and basically became a serial killer?"

"See, nobody's going to believe me."

"I didn't say I didn't believe you. I'm just—" Owen couldn't wrap his mind around this new knot in the thread of her story "—it's just hard to take it in." He got up off his knees and sank into the sofa again, putting his head in his hands. "He hired a hit man to kill you?" Saying it aloud, it sounded insane.

"It had to be him behind it, Owen. After Ladonna's warning, the guy mentioning Daisy Beech…" He heard her get to her feet but didn't look up; he was too shocked to move. "Grenville has everything to lose if I talk about what happened thirteen years ago. Ladonna and I… we're the only ones who know what he did."

He sat there, looking at her feet in the new shoes.

Finally he locked his fingers at the back of his neck and looked up. "I've got to ask you—why didn't you go to the police about him a long time ago?"

Her expression froze. "Are you interrogating me?"

"No, I'm trying to understand." He sat up, exhausted both mentally and emotionally. "But you've got to realize, if you ever come forward with all this, you're going to get a lot more embarrassing questions than that." He turned his palms out. "Benny, it's the nature of this kind of accusation."

"I don't know if a man can ever understand. The night I got away from Ladonna, the police caught her and charged her and she wound up serving time. There was a huge splash in the Memphis news. Because I was a minor, my picture was suppressed, but it was still awful—seeing photos and film of the place, pictures of Ladonna and the older girls. And I had to testify at her trial." She shivered.

Owen wanted badly to hold her, comfort her. But she had withdrawn completely into a shell. "I'm sure that was awful."

"You can't imagine. By that time, Grenville had faded off the scene. I never knew his name until later, when Ladonna told me who he was. She didn't turn on him… maybe he knew something else about her or maybe he'd threatened her. Certainly she was afraid of him. She hoped as long as she lay low he'd leave her alone.

"As for me, I just wanted to keep all that in the past, where it belonged. Focus on healing and getting my education and serving God." A heavy breath lifted her shoulders. "I'm just now seeing how cowardly that was. I should have laid myself out in the open to make him serve justice."

"Bernadette—" he stood up and approached her "—you are the bravest woman I've ever met."

But she backed away toward the window, where planes flew on and off the runways like bees around a hive. "We'll see how brave I am after I talk to Ladonna. I'm going to try to get her to corroborate my story. Then I'll go to the police."

Briggs perched in the woods outside Ladonna Sherman's—aka Sister Zena's—little house out in the sticks. Somebody had conveniently left a portable tree stand attached to a white oak tree, so he'd climbed up into it and settled down to wait. He wasn't much of a wildlife man. Didn't really like the taste of venison. But he enjoyed the thrill of the hunt.

He had taken care of one problem and it was just a matter of time before the other one was history.

Grenville himself could have found Carmichael and the girl if they'd flown commercial like normal people. But Briggs had been crawling the Internet, looking up flight plans, while he was stuck in that godforsaken little airport in Del Rio, Texas. Only one carrier out of it and his flight got canceled because the plane had had a mechanical problem. A night in some fleabag motel left him exhausted and cranky.

He slapped at a mosquito. Definitely cranky.

But he had already somewhat relieved his feelings this morning. Just a matter of time and he'd be all set for Acapulco. Or maybe Cancún. He'd just have to remember to buy sunscreen so his chemical peel wouldn't get infected by sun poison.

He could hardly believe how naive the girl was,

sticking her head into the oven this way. Carmichael had filed a flight plan with Wilson Air Center for this very day. Where he'd found a plane to charter was anybody's guess. Didn't matter. Grenville was convinced they were headed down here to connect with Zena. Briggs hoped so. He'd hate to think he'd wasted most of a day out here in the woods for nothing.

Owen talked Bernadette into letting him drive the rental car. He was way too jumpy to sit without something to occupy his hands. Exiting the airport, he circled I-240, merging onto I-55, and headed south across the Mississippi state line.

Benny sat beside him, hands loosely clasped in her lap, staring out the window at flat, boring delta.

Was she so shaken by what she'd told him that she was completely numb? He had no idea what to say, how to comfort her. So with a hard punch of his finger he turned on the radio and searched until he found a Christian station. A praise chorus filled the silence.

> "The Lord stood at my side
> And gave me strength,
> So that through me the message
> Might be fully proclaimed.
> And I was delivered
> From the lion's mouth.
> The Lord will rescue me
> From every attack
> And will bring me safely
> To His heavenly kingdom.

To Him be glory
Forever and ever. Amen."

Well, it beat the ode to rice pudding.

"Why are you smiling?" Bernadette was staring at him. "What are you thinking? You haven't said much since I told you—" she swallowed "—you know, all that at the airport."

"I was remembering your song about the paper from the king—'You have to marry my son, rice pudding.'"

"What?" She smiled. "Owen, you are so weird."

"I know." He sighed. "I'm just trying to absorb everything I know about you and piece it all back together into something I can deal with."

"How do you think I feel?"

"I can't imagine."

She fell silent and looked away.

How did a woman deal with the violation of her body, over and over, and emerge with unshakable maturity? What price of fear and anger and humiliation had she paid?

The ordeal he'd been through with his father paled in comparison.

Be honest, Carmichael. You're selfish. You look at her and imagine the parade of men who must have touched her before you. Men who paid to know her intimately.

Sickened all over again, he turned the radio up. Maybe to drown out his thoughts. But nothing would do that. As much as he wanted to forget it—realizing that those events had happened to her before he knew her—the truth, realistically, would touch their lives from now on.

Lord, can I accept it and still offer to be her husband? Can I love her as Christ loved the church, with self-sacrifice and purity? I'm just a man. I've never had a challenge like this one. The physical things I can do. Give me a plane or helicopter to fly. Give me a bad guy to take out and I'm Your man.

But why did You give me this woman to love?

Why, Lord?

"Are we getting close?"

Bernadette looked up at Owen from the satellite map printout she'd made back at the airport business center.

"I think so." If she'd remembered Ladonna's address incorrectly, this whole trip was a bust. Her memory was generally dependable, but what if she'd transposed a number or misspelled the name of the road?

But how many Duchovny Roads could there be in Coldwater, Mississippi?

She had spent a good part of her life in the rural South. This flat, wooded area where Ladonna had chosen to hide from Grenville seemed familiar, almost like home. Well, as much as any place could seem like home. They crossed a creek with a small concrete bridge, passed cotton fields and a long stand of woods covered in dormant brown kudzu. In just another month, the parasitic vines would be green and growing with ferocious vitality.

"Owen, I'm not sure it's a good idea for you to come to Ladonna's house."

"Why not? I've come all this way."

"She'll be upset that I brought somebody with me. She's very private these days."

He frowned. "I'm not letting you go by yourself. In fact, I've been thinking. If we can figure out a back way in there, we'll take it."

She blinked. "Why?" The vague anxiety that had lurked all day suddenly turned into gut-clenching fear. "Do you think they followed us?"

"I didn't see anybody behind us, and I've been watching. But I can't help thinking it's a possibility. If Grenville suspects you might have been headed to meet with the woman after you left Mexico—"

"There's no reason he'd know that. There was that e-mail on the Garretts' computer back in Agrexco. But he couldn't possibly have seen that."

"Bernadette, you said this guy is ruthless, and I believe you. He does have a lot at stake. Have you considered that if he found you after you'd changed your name and moved to Mexico, he could also find this Sherman woman? Especially since she's right here, close to her old stomping grounds."

"I don't know." She crumpled the paper in her lap, then smoothed it against her legs. "Maybe he did find her and has been just biding his time. I know Ladonna was alive until at least six days ago, when I got her e-mail."

"Anything could happen in six days."

"The walls of Jericho fell down in six days." She hadn't meant to sound sarcastic, but the thought popped out of her mouth before she could stop it. She'd fallen in love with Owen in six days, too.

Yeah, the walls were down and there was no putting them back up.

Owen gave her an inscrutable look. "Just to be safe, tell

me where the next turn is. We'll go down one more road and see if we can double back from behind her house."

"All right. Look for Duchovny Road, maybe another quarter of a mile." They passed a couple of barns, the highway twisted to the left and she saw a green road marker at the top of a shallow rise. "There. I think that's it."

Owen slowed. "Yeah. Okay, can you tell from the map if there's another turn off the highway?"

"Yes. Half a mile down."

They followed the highway past a small brick church with a cemetery, then slowed at another road marker to the left. "Let me look at the map." He studied it, nodded and handed it back to her. "This'll work."

Within five seconds, Bernadette had no idea where she was, but Owen apparently had some internal GPS that kept him going in the right direction. He drove with single-minded confidence through a maze of kudzu and cotton-lined backcountry roads.

After a couple of minutes, he said triumphantly, "Ha. This is it. We're at the neighbor's house behind her place."

"Are you sure? How do you know?" She looked at him in amazement.

"Your gift is language, mine is sense of direction." He pulled onto a tiny dirt road that led into a soybean field, braked and turned off the ignition. About fifty yards away, at the end of the field, a stand of woods marched toward the horizon.

Bernadette took a deep breath and opened the car door. "All right. I trust you're right. Let's go."

She followed him across the field, stepping over the rows of greening young plants. The woods started as a thin scattering of white oak and pine, with a scrubby underbrush of briers, magnolia and dogwood. Gradually, it thickened until they were dodging trees with every step.

She snagged her foot on a thorny tangle of vines and stopped to untangle herself. "Owen, wait a sec...." Her ankle was bleeding and mosquitoes swarmed around her head.

A few steps ahead, he turned. When he saw her difficulty, he retraced his steps, crouched and gently pulled the stickers out of her jeans. Holding her foot in his hand, he looked up with a rueful smile. "Sorry. I get too focused when I'm on a trail." He examined the welling scratch. "We'll put some ointment on that when we get out of here. Let's keep going before the skeeters eat us alive."

Standing up, he took her hand and made sure she stayed with him until the woods began to thin again. He drew her to a halt and placed a finger across his lips. "Quiet from here on," he whispered.

Walking as slowly and silently as possible, Bernadette copied Owen's movements. Another minute or so later, she saw a little white house through the trees and, beyond it, as they got closer, an outbuilding with a four-wheel ATV parked in its gravel driveway. A butane tank squatted in the yard beside a pumphouse with a spigot and hose.

The place looked like Ladonna's description of her home. Bernadette's admiration of Owen's scouting abilities soared.

But when she would have walked out of the woods into the yard, he held her back. "Shh," he breathed into her ear. "I'm going first. Just follow me."

He padded along the edge of the woods, drawing her by the hand behind him, until they were just five yards from the back side of the outbuilding, at its closest point to the trees.

"All right, let me go first. Watch for me to tell you when." He ran for the building, keeping his body low. When nothing happened—not a sound except the twittering of some wrens along the eaves of the roof—he motioned for Bernadette to join him.

She followed, feeling almost silly with all this skulking around. *Nobody's here except Ladonna.*

But her heart insisted on pounding. She inched along the back of the shed behind Owen, stopping at the corner. He ducked, ran for the big silver butane tank and crouched behind it. After a moment, he waved her toward him.

The back entrance of the house—a French door in a screened porch—was about ten yards away. Ladonna was going to have a heart attack when two strangers showed up without warning. It was such a pretty spring afternoon. Seemed like a shame they couldn't park in the driveway and walk up to the front door like long lost friends.

Owen's mouth was at her ear again. "You ready?" he whispered.

Shivering, she nodded and they ran for the porch. Owen tried the handle and went in first.

Please, Lord, don't let us scare Ladonna.

She stood there holding Owen's hand, listening to utter silence. The refrigerator kicked on in the kitchen nearby, rattling something on top of it.

"Ladonna?" Bernadette called softly. Something didn't feel right. If Ladonna was here, there should be some noise somewhere. Maybe she'd walked down to a neighbor's house. Or maybe she was asleep. She tugged at Owen's hand when he started for the kitchen. "This time *you* wait here. Let me look for her. I don't want to frighten her."

He shook his head, but she dropped his hand and walked into the kitchen before he could stop her.

"Ladonna? It's Bernadette. I've come all the way from Mexico to see you." She walked as she talked, looking into the breakfast nook off the kitchen, then a tiny formal living room. The furnishings were spare and old-fashioned, and posters with Christian messages were tacked with straight pins on the walls. No hint of the mystical practices that used to occupy her time back on Beale Street.

Thank you, Lord, for that!

Down a short hallway on the other side of the living room, she passed a bathroom and a bedroom without seeing Ladonna. So strange to walk through the woman's house when she wasn't here. But maybe she could figure out where she'd been, or at least leave a note so she could get in touch later.

The last room on the left was a bedroom. Maybe she was taking a nap. "Ladonna?" Shag carpet, a quilted bedspread and thick draperies deadened the sound of her footsteps. The bed was empty.

Not right. She ought to be here. A door opened off the bedroom—probably a second bath. Okay, one more place to look.

She walked past the bed, glanced down at something draped across the floor.

SIXTEEN

Briggs heard the scream and nearly fell out of the tree stand. *How did they get past me?*

Shouldering the gun, he struggled to climb down without falling. The nylon straps attached to the platform were old and rotten. It didn't take him long to realize that if he moved too fast he was going to drop twenty feet to the ground and break his neck.

Normally, heights didn't bother him, but his anxiety to get to the girl made him miss the first step. Catching his foot on the second step, he grabbed the steel hoop that hooked around the tree trunk.

Whew, that was close. Confident now, he descended two more steps. Then the third one broke.

Tumbling, he hit the ground with a heavy thud, the breath knocked out of him.

"Benny!" Owen tore through the house, heart crashing. Just that one scream and she'd gone silent. What had happened?

He reached the hallway and heard her sobbing. Where was she? The front bedroom? *Oh, God, please not—*

There she was, kneeling by the bed, where a pool of blood stained the carpet. A middle-aged woman lay face up under the shattered window, her heavyset body covered in glass. Long dyed-blond hair trailed across the floor.

The blood came from the back of her head, where a bullet had exited from the ragged hole in her forehead.

Bernadette turned to look at him, her tear-streaked face blanched to chalky gray. Horror darkened her eyes, turned her breath to loud panting.

"Owen!" she wailed. "Look what they did!"

Oh, man. What now? He wasn't armed. The killer could be outside looking for them. He'd done the right thing, entering the house carefully, but with Bernadette's scream, they would know right where they were.

"We've gotta get out of here." He bent and tried to lift her. "We've got to get away safe and then call the police."

"No, she's—she's dead. I can't just leave her!" She reached toward the woman's slack face. "Ladonna…"

"Bernadette, don't touch her!" Owen crouched and laid his hand against her wet cheek, making her look at him. "Give me your eyes." She reluctantly focused on him. "We have *got* to go."

"Why?"

She wasn't sentient. How was he going to get her out of here? "I promise we'll come back. Come on, baby, take my hand."

Blinking a couple of times, she smeared her hand under her nose and let him help her up. "Where are we going?"

"Back to the car. We're gonna go call the police."

"Right." Holding his hand, she followed him, looking back as they reached the bedroom door. She began to shake so violently he could feel the tremors up his arm.

"Hold on. It'll be okay." It wasn't okay. They were in a mess. Their footprints were all over this murder scene.

They were at the screen porch door when he heard a noise from the front, through the shattered window. Owen shoved Bernadette through the door and flung himself after her. A shot blasted outside the house. Had the shooter seen them? Grabbing Bernadette's hand, he ran with her across the yard.

Lord, my Savior! Help us!

They made it to the butane tank and ducked behind it.

Another gunshot blasted from somewhere, but it sounded like a wild shot. Maybe the guy still hadn't seen them.

Back the way they'd come—the only thing to do.

He put his hands on either side of Benny's face. "Listen." He kept his voice quiet but urgent. "We're going to run back through the woods, but we've got to stay quiet. Okay?" Her eyes were still blank, inward. He knew shock when he saw it. "Benny!" Brushing his thumbs over her cheeks, he kissed her quickly. "Are you hearing me?"

She blinked and nodded.

They couldn't wait here any longer. "Let's go."

Stooping, he pulled her with him toward the shed. Distant running footfalls crashed through the trees on the other side of the house. They made it to the back of the shed, crossing the last five feet of open space as they dodged into the woods.

"Benny, I need you to go on to the car. I'll be right behind you." He hoped to get a look at the shooter's face. God forbid, if something happened to Bernadette, he wanted to be able to identify the scum.

For a second he thought she might balk, but with a muffled groan, she obeyed and took off.

Lord, he prayed as he crouched behind a slender oak, *help her get back without getting lost.* He was close enough to get a view of the clearing but safely hidden by trees and underbrush. Seconds, or even minutes—he didn't know how much—later, a dark, heavily muscled man in camouflage pants and T-shirt ran around the side of the house.

Panting, the man stopped to search the quiet yard, the butt of the gun at his shoulder. He slowly scoped the barrel first in one direction, then the other.

Owen had seen enough. Melting into the woods, he took off after Bernadette. Most of his recent work had been in the rolling south Texas hills, the desert or along the river—and mainly in the air. But long weeks of training came back as he ran for the car. Heel to toe, zig-zagging, avoiding fallen branches that might crack underfoot. Soft and fast. Farther and deeper into the woods until he was halfway.

Please, God, let Bernadette be waiting for me.

The trees began to thin. He saw the car, and she was in it. *Thank You....*

Making a hard dash across the soybean field, he glanced over his shoulder. Their pursuer was nowhere in sight. God had preserved them. He got in the car, where Bernadette sat hunched over with her face in her hands.

"It's okay," he said helplessly as he started the engine and backed wildly down the little tractor road. "It's gonna be okay."

She didn't answer, just shuddered.

Twisting along the snaking backcountry roads at a

reckless speed, Owen tried to figure out what to do now. Call the police, obviously. Send them to the murder scene.

He had to take care of Bernadette, too. Maybe take her to an emergency room. No, they couldn't take a chance on being seen at obvious places as long as the assassin was on the loose.

Where? Where could he take her? Someplace they could rest, assess the situation, be safe.

Turning onto the main highway, he drove half a mile and saw the cemetery and the little white church sitting on its hill. *Okay. Yeah. That'll work. Lord, please don't let it be locked.*

A small paved parking lot, completely empty on this weekday afternoon, extended beside the sanctuary and ran under an overhang to the back of the building. Owen followed the pavement until it came to an end and turned off onto the grass behind a play yard. He couldn't see the road from here, which meant they were safely hidden. Turning off the ignition, he looked at his hands on the steering wheel. He couldn't believe they were steady. His heart was racing like an Olympic sprinter.

"Bernadette?" He reached out and laid his hand between her shoulder blades. She jerked. "We're safe. We're at a church. We're gonna hide out here 'til we figure out what to do."

"Okay." To his surprise, she lowered her hands. But her eyes were still closed, her face red from weeping. "I can't believe it. He killed her, too. How did he find her?"

"I don't know. But let's go inside and we'll call for help."

He went around, opened her door and helped her

out. Together they ran up a set of concrete steps to a back door. It was locked. Disappointed but not surprised, Owen touched Bernadette's shoulder. "Wait here. I'll check the front door."

Cautiously, dreading the thought of being out in the open when the gunman could drive by, he stayed close to the building as he went around to the front. A broad sweep of curved steps led to a set of double doors. Locked, as well.

Now what?

Jogging back to rejoin Bernadette, he continued to pray, trying not to despair. God had delivered them from so many tight spots already. They had to put faith in action again.

He rounded the back corner of the building and nearly had heart failure when he didn't see her. Where had she gone?

"Bernadette?"

Suddenly the church's back door opened. Benny stuck her head out. "Owen! Come here. I found the prayer-room key under the mat."

"How did you know it was a prayer room?"

Benny, seated beside Owen on the cushioned front pew, shrugged. "This is just like the church I went to with the Coker family. It seemed like a good idea to check for a key. People are trusting."

She still hadn't gotten control of the tremors that shook her body, but normalcy was beginning to return. As normal as things could be when you'd witnessed the aftermath of a violent murder. Unexpected tears welled again. Maybe she'd never quit crying.

Owen slipped his arm around her shoulders and pulled her to him. "Do you want to talk about it?"

"Not yet." If she talked about it, she might fall apart again.

"Hey. I told you, we're safe here. He'll assume we got far away as fast as we could."

But she couldn't relax. "Have you called the police yet?"

"No. This guy's been chasing us across international borders. He could be mixed up in something a lot bigger than this one murder. I'm thinking we should call Jack Torres first. He'll be able to help us. Also, my buddy Johnny Stapp with the FBI."

"Owen, I'm so scared. With Ladonna dead, there's nobody to back up my story."

"That's why we go to somebody who knows you. Jack will make sure we get the right people involved." He paused and she looked up into concerned blue eyes. "You've got to be willing to talk now, Bernadette."

"I'm not running anymore," she said grimly. "Paul Grenville has terrorized me long enough. Call Jack."

Alone in the dark, Benny curled up on a pew with her shoes off and tried to pray herself to sleep. The musty little sanctuary was utterly silent and still, the air-conditioning evidently turned off during the week. She listened for mice in the attic but heard nothing.

Owen had insisted on sleeping in the car. She'd tried to tell him how ridiculous that was. Who would know whether or not he slept on a pew on the other side of the room?

"I promised I'd take care of your reputation," he'd

said stubbornly. "I keep my promises. Now lock the door behind me."

And he'd kissed her quickly on the forehead before heading outdoors.

So here she lay, lonely and scared and wanting to be held. If this was what it felt like to be in love, *no thanks*.

Owen hadn't said another word about his feelings since learning who she really was. Even that little good-night peck had been more comforting than romantic. He was drawing back from her, and there was nothing she could do about it.

All right, then. You've been a strong woman of God for a long time. Since when did you get so needy?

She wasn't needy. She'd been trying to convince people for years—Roxanne, Meg, Eli and Isabel—that she didn't need a man's love and protection to be complete. The Lord was enough. He *had* to be enough, as much as she loved Owen and wanted him.

Lord, it was good to get my walls broken down so that I could love somebody like that. Let the pain make me love You more. Let it make me love other people more. Help me bear it. Help me carry through with whatever You have for me tomorrow, and let Your will be done. Please help Owen, Jack and Johnny know what's best to do. In Jesus' name...

She relaxed, more at peace than she'd been since walking into that bloody, glass-strewn bedroom this afternoon. They *had* to make sure Ladonna's killer paid the price. Jack was flying down from Washington tomorrow, and Owen's old fraternity brother, Johnny Stapp, was coming up from San Antonio.

Surely they could figure out some way out of this mess.

* * *

"I don't know where they came from and I don't know where they went," Briggs told the judge as he drove to the airport.

Contract or no contract, he was headed to South America today. He figured there'd be a contract on *his* head by tonight.

"But she was there in the house? She knows Zena's dead?"

"It had to be her." Briggs passed the interstate exit sign for Graceland. Too bad he didn't have time to do the tour while he was in town. "After I lost them, I went inside the house and found bloody footprints tracked from the bedroom out to the screen porch."

"What'd you do then?"

"Figured they'd head back to the airport, so I checked on that. No dice. The plane they came in on is still there. So they either left commercial or drove out another way."

"Maybe she stuck around," Grenville speculated.

"Nah. I heard her scream. She got out of there as fast as her legs would take her."

"But if she was with the Border Patrol guy, no telling what she's up to. After all, they got past you and made it all the way to Memphis."

"I suppose." Briggs hated having his nose smeared in it.

"Look, Briggs, lay low here in Memphis until I need you."

"I don't know, boss—"

"Briggs, I'm telling you, if you leave town right now, I'll have you hunted down and snuffed like a cheap candle. You got me?"

"Yes, sir," Briggs said unhappily. "I got you."

* * *

Tuesday afternoon, the three law officers—Owen, Jack and Johnny—plus Bernadette met in a small conference room in a south Memphis hotel. They were joined by an African-American local agent named Duncan Osborn.

Owen studied Jack Torres with interest. He hadn't seen Torres in three years and marriage had changed the guy beyond recognition. Gone was the edgy, cynical hothead who used to be first up for the most dangerous assignments on the Texas border. Though still tall and fit, Jack now wore his black hair clipped short and neat. He'd lost his earring and the scruffy beard that had characterized his undercover jobs, and he wore a black dress shirt with gray slacks and an expensive leather belt. Homeland Security apparently enforced a dress code.

The physical was only part of the difference, though. Torres greeted Bernadette with strong, brotherly affection, letting her cry a little on his shoulder before setting her back and handing her a clean handkerchief from his back pocket. "I've learned to carry one," he said with a smile. "Meg cries all the time now that she's pregnant."

"Meg's pregnant?" Benny's face lit. "You're going to have a baby?"

"Well, yeah, I'm sorta involved." Jack grinned. "Did she not tell you? She'll kill me because she likes to tell people herself."

"How long have you known?" Benny clapped her hands.

"Congratulations, man." Owen took a seat at the

table, glad to see Bernadette so excited in spite of the trouble hanging over their heads.

"We found out a couple of weeks ago." Jack sat down across from Owen. "She's been pretty sick, so she may not have felt like making phone calls."

"I'm going for a cup of coffee before we get started." Osborn, the only one on his home turf, paused in the doorway. "Would anybody else like some?"

"I would," said Torres.

"Me, too. I'll help you bring it." Bernadette followed Osborn out.

Stapp opened a file on the table and sat down. He glanced at the door through which Benny had disappeared. "Owen, are you sure she's on the level about Judge Grenville? That's a mighty wild tale she's telling."

Owen frowned at his college friend. Over the years, Stapp had evolved from wild frat boy to brilliant, hard-as-nails investigative agent. Dressed in the obligatory dark suit and tie, clean-cut and buttoned-down, he was seriousness embodied.

"Johnny, the guy tried to kill her yesterday."

Stapp rubbed his forehead with two fingers. "So far we don't have any connection between the attack on the Sherman woman and the judge. We've got guys down there right now collecting evidence and photographing the scene. But it'll take time to analyze all that, subpoena phone records and go through them."

"And in the meantime, Bernadette is a walking target!" Owen had trouble containing his frustration. "I need you guys to help me protect her."

"We will." Jack sat relaxed in his chair. "You know we don't want anything to happen to her."

Stapp nodded. "Isn't there anybody else besides her who can corroborate what she says about the judge soliciting young prostitutes all those years ago? If we can nail him for rape, we'd have an easier time getting hold of the other records before he has time to destroy them."

Listening to his friends discuss Bernadette in this clinical way was excruciating. "No, because he already murdered the other three girls who were involved. Benny says she's the only one left."

"Owen, I know this is hard." Jack regarded him with sympathetic eyes. "But remember, we're not the antagonists."

Owen took a deep breath. "You're right. I just, well, you know how I feel about her."

Torres nodded. "Yeah. We'll come up with something." He smiled at Bernadette as she came in the room carrying a tray full of coffee cups. "Looks like you hit the jackpot."

"There's a nice espresso bar in there." She helped Osborn serve the other men, avoiding Owen's eyes as she set a cup in front of him. "I put sugar in yours."

"Thanks."

Her attitude today left him all off balance. She seemed to have left behind the catatonic state she'd been in right after they'd discovered Ladonna's body and escaped the shooter. When he'd knocked on the church door this morning, she'd greeted him with calm reserve.

Why was she shutting him out, after everything they'd been through?

Maybe he'd been a little cool with her last night, but he couldn't have taken a night spent in the same room with her, no matter what she said. He'd wanted to hold her so badly, he'd had to forcibly remove himself to the discomforts of the backseat of the car.

It had been a miserable, mosquito-infested night.

Bernadette sat down beside Jack and leaned into him. Torres put his arm around her; she seemed to absorb the comfort of her best friend's husband's shoulder.

Owen looked away. Bernadette deserved a little comfort in the situation. He just wished he had the right to be the one giving it.

SEVENTEEN

Bernadette could tell that Owen didn't want to be here. He and Jack were friends, but something seemed to have happened while she was out of the room. He had gone quiet, and generally Owen always had something to say.

It wasn't her fault if he had a crick in his neck. *He* was the one who'd insisted on sleeping in the car.

Hearing Johnny Stapp mention her name, she blinked, tuning back in to the conversation. Everyone was looking at her. "I'm sorry, what did you say?"

"I just spent fifteen minutes explaining my idea," said Stapp on a plaintive note, "and I'm going to have to say it again?"

"Please."

"You FBI guys have a talent for beating around the bush," said Jack dryly. "I can say it in one sentence. Benny, we want you to set up a meeting with Grenville and wear a wire."

"Is *that* what he was saying?" Owen shoved back his chair. "No way."

"Come on, Carmichael." Stapp looked impatient. "You want us to catch the guy, don't you?"

"Yeah, but she's a civilian. She's never worn a wire. She's not trained for this kind of thing and she'll get herself killed. No way," he repeated.

"We'll have her surrounded by our guys. She's smarter than all four of us put together." Jack winked at her. "Aren't you, Benny?"

She jerked up her chin. "I certainly am." The idea of facing Grenville after all these years, after everything he'd done, made her physically ill. But she wasn't going to let Owen tell her what she couldn't do.

"It's not a matter of brains." Owen folded his arms. "I'm well aware of her intelligence. This is about experience. And the fact that she's afraid of this guy, which will make her nervous and create potential mistakes."

"*She* is right here," Benny fired at him, "and I can speak for myself. Don't treat me like an idiot." Echoing words he'd said to her not so long ago gave her a jagged kind of satisfaction.

As if against his will, his gaze clashed with hers. She suddenly saw the stark fear in the deep-water blue of his eyes. Her lips parted.

"I'm not treating you like an idiot," he said before she could speak. "I'm treating you like the woman I love." He looked at Jack. "You've gotta find another way to get this guy. You're not sending my girl to meet with him."

Stapp and Osborn both looked uncomfortable, but Jack shifted his shoulders and dug in. "Stapp's right, Owen. If Benny's the only living witness, then our best shot at nailing him is to get him on tape."

"I've seen the hit man," Owen said. "Use me."

"We'll let you be there to identify the guy if he happens to show up. But Grenville's the one we really want. He wouldn't talk to anybody but her."

"You don't know that."

Jack's expression was compassionate. He'd faced putting his wife in similar danger three years ago, before they married. "You know it's the truth."

Owen cracked his knuckles. Benny waited for him to look at her again. He didn't have the right to command her one way or the other, and he knew it. Did he really love her, or was he just being stubborn and macho? She hoped she knew the answer to that question, but fear threatened to consume her.

Slowly Owen got to his feet. "Can Benny and I talk somewhere alone before she decides?"

"You don't have much time." Stapp checked his watch. "If we're gonna do this tomorrow, I've got to get my guys lined up."

"Bernadette." Owen caught her eyes again. "Will you come talk to me for just a minute? I promise I won't take long."

She managed a jerky nod and looked at Stapp as she walked toward the door. "We'll be right back."

"All right, but Owen—" Stapp tapped the file on the table. "Hurry, man."

The coffee room was empty. Owen shut the door and leaned against it.

Benny crossed over to a table against the wall and faced him. "You can't tell me what to do."

"I know it." He looked miserable.

"This is my chance to put this criminal away for good."

"I know that, too."

"Then what is your *problem?* I'm not afraid of him." She was, but Owen didn't have to know.

"Bernadette, this is not about your ability, your bravery, your intelligence or any of that. It's about the fact that if I lose you—" He pushed his hand through his streaked hair and closed his eyes. "Anything I say is going to sound melodramatic and stupid! How can I tell you what you mean to me? I love you more than life."

When he looked at her again, she was shocked to see tears standing in his eyes, making them look like brilliant gems in his sun-browned face.

"Owen—"

"This isn't the time or place to deal with this, but will you please think about that before you go throwing yourself to the wolves?"

Think about it? After everything she'd told him, after all the danger she'd put him in, he still loved her. But he wanted her to be a coward.

"I can't." She gripped the counter behind her. "I can't think about it because I have to do what they say. I can't let him get away with what he did."

"There's got to be another way."

"No. Move out of my way, Owen. They're waiting for me."

He stood there for nearly a minute, feet planted apart, as she faced him down. Finally she walked right up to him, pushed him out of the way and opened the door.

And he let her.

Grenville scowled when Marjorie answered the phone in the middle of a Wednesday night bridge game with their next-door neighbors.

He had come home to Memphis for a fund-raiser scheduled for the weekend. The press conferences in Washington had gone well. Everybody in the White House was impressed with his record on all the important issues. His motto: Walk straight down the middle, with a slight lean to the right. And now it had paid off. He was a media darling at the moment.

Of course, it could all come crashing down if the McBride girl opened her mouth at the wrong time. Briggs was still looking for her, but Grenville wasn't worried. Briggs had had a lot of bad luck, but he was good at tracking.

"Marjorie," he said with a teasing wink at pretty young Daria Price, "tell the state troopers I'll donate to the charity gospel sing, or whatever it is they're soliciting for, but get off the phone. It's your turn to bid." Daria giggled as he picked up his iced tea glass and rattled the glass. "And bring the pitcher back to the table while you're up, would you?"

Marjorie wandered over with the cordless phone pressed to her shoulder. "It's not the state troopers." She always took him literally. There was a puzzled frown between her eyes. "There's a young woman on the line who says she knew you when she was a teenager. She wants to speak to you."

Grenville felt his mouth go dry. "I'll take the call." He laid his cards down, jarring the table with his thighs as he jerked to his feet. "Be right back," he mumbled to Marjorie on the way to the study.

"Hello?" He heard the extension click as Marjorie hung it up. Rage building in the back of his neck, he sank into his executive chair. "Who is this?"

"You know who it is," she said in the honey-sweet tones of a confident, well-brought-up, young Southern lady. "You've been hunting me down for over a week."

"Where are you?"

"I'm not telling you." She sounded nervous now. "But I'm someplace you can't find me until I get ready to be found." She paused, then blurted, "I have something that might interest you."

"What's that?" he asked through clenched teeth. How dare she call him at home and talk to his wife?

"Did you think you got rid of all the evidence when you murdered Ladonna?" Her voice got a little stronger with anger. "And Daisy and Tamika and Celine? I know about those three because Ladonna told me. And she warned me you might come after me."

"You are crazy, you little—" He called her what she was. "I didn't murder anybody."

"You can call me names," she said calmly, "but I'm not what I was before. I belong to Jesus now, and you can't ever snatch me away."

"I don't care who you belong to. What's this about evidence? You think anybody's going to believe what you say?"

"As they say, seeing is believing."

Sucker punched, he waited until he got his breath back. "I don't have any idea what you're talking about."

"Ladonna had cameras in her house. She left some tapes and I took one with me when I was there."

"You're lying."

"Like I said, seeing is proof. I could hardly make something like that up."

"I won't be blackmailed, and I can't believe you'd actually put yourself in that kind of media spotlight."

"I don't want money. You're right—all I want is to be left alone. And all you want is power. We can both have what we want. I'll bring you a copy of the tape so you can see I'm telling you the truth. As long I never see or hear from you again, the tape stays in my safety deposit box. You touch me again and I'll make sure you're exposed for the monster you are. How does that sound?"

"Interesting. You can mail me the copy."

"No. I'll hand it to you personally."

"Why? Surely you don't want to see me again that badly."

Silence. Then she said slowly, "I'll hand it to you face-to-face or not at all. I just want you to leave me alone, Judge Grenville."

He sighed. "I'm in the middle of something important. When and where do you want to meet?"

"Tomorrow morning at Overton Park. There's a public picnic area outside the zoo. Meet me there at ten o'clock."

"All right. But don't call me here again."

"After tomorrow, I won't have to."

A dial tone buzzed in his ear.

"Did you get that?" asked Stapp. He looked at Osborn, who was operating the recorder set up on the conference table.

With a shaking hand, Benny put down the phone. Now that she'd set up the meeting, she felt like rushing for the ladies' room to vomit. Hearing that deep, hateful voice brought back memories she had no desire to revisit.

"I got it." Osborn adjusted his headphones and rewound the tape. "It's not enough for a warrant, though."

Stapp, seated beside Benny, patted her wrist. "You did fine, Bernadette. I'm proud of you."

She glanced at Owen, who sat in a chair across the room. His fists were clenched between his knees, his brow knit as he watched her. Catching her gaze, he nodded stiffly.

"You're gonna do great. We'll all be there with you."

"Men in Black, we got you covered," said Stapp with a teasing glint in his eyes.

"What kills me is a guy like this gets in a position of power without anybody knowing who he really is." Osborn listened to the tape. "What a creep."

"It happens all the time." Owen looked at the young agent, cynicism coloring his expression. "I had firsthand experience growing up with the ultimate heroic father, husband, lawman. Selfishness took over and he wouldn't turn back to God. Ruined his life."

"And lots of others." Jack met Owen's eyes. "But God can do His will and bring good out of the worst situations. Even this one." He looked at Benny. "You believe that, Benny?"

"I do. I've seen it before." She wanted to get up and go to Owen. He was clearly struggling to reconcile himself with what she had to do. But she had to leave him alone to wrestle this out with God. "I can trust the Lord to do what's best for me."

Owen stared at her, the connection between them arcing like an electrical current. She didn't have to physically touch him; he knew her heart.

* * *

Wednesday morning, Benny woke up in the hotel room with a start. She'd been dreaming all night.

Nightmares about the little attic room at Ladonna's house. Spiders building webs across the ceiling. The lumpy futon on the floor and the pitiful stack of Bibles in the corner.

The bars she used to frequent, scouting out tricks.

Ladonna's ravaged, manipulative face and the little knife she kept in her pocket to keep the girls in line.

Sweating, she threw back the sheet and hurried for the shower. She was supposed to meet the FBI agents downstairs at eight. They were going to go over her instructions one more time and fix her up with the wire.

Maybe Owen would pray with her before she went to the park.

Dressed in Isabel's sundress, which she'd insisted on giving her, she walked into the breakfast lounge. As if her thinking about him had conjured him up, Owen sat at a little table by the window, reading the paper. His eyes looked glassy.

She met his gaze for a second, then fixed herself a cup of orange juice before approaching him. She didn't feel like eating.

"Want some company?"

Owen put the paper on a nearby table and sighed. "Sure."

"Did you sleep last night?"

"Not much. You?"

She sipped her juice. "A little. Had nightmares."

"You don't have to do this, Bernadette."

"Owen, don't."

"All right." He rubbed his forehead. "I've been praying for you all night."

"That's good. Will you pray with me now?"

"If you want me to." He looked around. "We'd better stay here in the open."

Disappointed, she bowed her head. "Okay. You lead."

Wearing a University of Memphis baseball cap and jacket, a camo T-shirt and disreputable jeans, Owen waited with another undercover agent inside the ticket booth of the Overton Park Zoo. On a beautiful spring day in the middle of the week, there was nobody here but day-care tour groups and a few senior citizens with season passes. He hoped they'd be able to keep civilians out of the action.

Through Osborn's binoculars, he watched Bernadette get out of the little white rental car in the parking lot. All alone. In the yellow sundress and denim jacket, with her hair twisted into a conservative knot at the back of her head, she looked beautiful and vulnerable.

Why did I let her do this? Lord, if we ever get married…

If they got through this and got married, she'd have him wrapped around her finger. She could do whatever she wanted and he'd kiss her feet.

The thought almost made him smile.

Not *if* they got married. *When.*

But his stomach still roiled as if he were on a ship in a high storm. What if Grenville had a hit man somewhere and Johnny's guys didn't find him? What if the snake somehow slithered out of the trap without incriminating himself? What if Bernadette let something slip and Grenville discovered there was no tape?

They'd be right back where they started, with Bernadette in mortal danger—and with him over here so far away he couldn't protect her. All he could do was pray with every breath. And worry.

At ten minutes to ten, Bernadette reached the zoo entrance, where a series of enormous concrete animal statues greeted visitors. She walked up to the lion and leaned back against it, absorbing strength from what it represented. More than just a tourist attraction or photo op. She closed her eyes.

Lion of Judah, holy Lord. My Father and protector. Please keep me safe in Your hands. Give me the right words and help me not give in to fear. Let Your will be done. Let justice be done.

She looked around, suddenly calm. Owen was here somewhere. Watching and worrying. She'd seen the love in his eyes this morning and that helped give her confidence.

What would I do without him, Lord?

She couldn't think about that right now. *Concentrate on your instructions. Get this over with.*

The time for running away was done.

Taking a deep breath, she walked over to the picnic area, which was outside the zoo in an area shaded by huge, arching oaks. In a city as hot and humid as Memphis, the trees were an invaluable resource. Especially with all this concrete and pavement baking in the sun.

She chose the third picnic table past the parking lot. It was fairly clean, in spite of the bird population. This early in the morning there was little trash littering the grass. She sat down on the concrete bench, placed her new handbag in her lap and folded her hands on top of it. It contained the fake VHS tape the feds had given her.

Please, God, let him believe me. All those times he lied to his wife and his family. All the lies he's told to people who trust him to be a fair judge. If You want to bring him to repentance later that's fine with me, but right now, Lord, please do justice.

She looked up and saw him getting out of his car. It was a red convertible sports car with the top down.

He hadn't changed much over the years. Still tall and slim—he'd bragged about being a college basketball star—with thick gray hair and expensive sunglasses. Well-fitted casual clothes. The look of power.

Why a man like that had been consumed with seducing teenage girls continued to mystify her.

It was a struggle not to look down at the tiny microphone lodged in the pocket of her jacket. Her hands clenched her purse. Where were the agents assigned to her? She'd been told they would sweep the area during the night and stay in place until her meeting with Grenville took place.

Defiantly, she sat where she was, refusing to rise in the judge's presence as he approached.

He stopped a few feet away and let his gaze sweep her figure, head to toe. "You're looking well."

"I'm fine." What did you say to the man who destroyed your childhood?

The Lord is the strength of my life. My light and my salvation.

She didn't want to talk to him, but she had to get him to say out loud what he'd done.

He sat down at the opposite end of the picnic table. "Thank you for not saying anything to my wife last night."

Apparently he was going to go for conciliation. Okay, fine.

"She didn't do anything wrong. I can't believe she never knew about you."

"There's nothing for her to know. I'm a good husband and father. I'm a generous provider."

He hadn't admitted anything, but in a flash, she realized that pride was his Achilles' heel.

"You used to provide for me and Daisy and the others."

"You were the prettiest one." His tone was almost avuncular.

She wanted to scratch his eyes out.

"It hurt when you left me in the Peabody that day. That was the day I left Ladonna's house."

"Come on. Surely you had other providers."

"None like you." Bile rose in her throat and she swallowed it. "I was never going to tell on you. Why did you send that man to kill me?"

EIGHTEEN

Inside the ticket booth, Owen struggled with rage so deep he wondered if he'd ever get over it. Nothing could have prepared him to watch this: the man who had violated his love—his sweetheart, his Bernadette—sitting beside her at a picnic table, in conversation as if he were a long lost friend.

They hadn't let him wait in the van with the sound equipment, where he could have worn headphones and heard every word. So he was stuck here watching through the binoculars like a monkey in a cage.

Unable to stomach the sight any longer, he moved the binoculars. Something crossed his vision, a tourist entering the plaza in front of the zoo. The glasses case jerked in his hands and he refocused. The man was gone, apparently disappearing beside the fence. Owen searched again and found him, a man in a fishing hat and unremarkable clothes: a plaid shirt, khakis and sneakers. Limping along the fence with his hands in his pockets, he looked toward the picnic area.

He had a large Italian nose, florid skin and heavy shoulders.

Owen's pulse roared in his ears. "Stapp, the hit man's here."

"Where?"

"Near the fence. The guy in the fishing hat. I'm going after him."

"Carmichael, we've got agents already out there. We'll radio one of them to take the guy out."

"You can do that, but I'm going, too."

Before Stapp could do more than mutter a brief expletive and pick up his radio, Owen was out the door and rounding the outside of the ticket booth. Slouching along the fence in the direction he'd seen the hit man heading, he tugged his cap lower to hide his face. There was no way he was sitting tamely in a ticket booth when this guy was setting up to kill Bernadette.

"It was nothing personal," said Grenville. He brushed a leaf off the table, then leaned an elbow on it. "The other girls had threatened to talk, so I assumed you would, too." He gave her a thoughtful stare. "Apparently, you have a little more to lose in the way of reputation. I was…surprised to hear you'd become a missionary. I'll have Marjorie send a donation to the orphanage."

She gaped at him in utter revulsion. "I don't want your money." She pulled the tape out of her purse with unsteady hands and slid it across the table. "This is enough to convict you on any number of nasty charges if I ever decide to use it."

"How enterprising of Zena to hold on to this all these years. I imagine she planned to blackmail me, too." He sighed and placed perfectly manicured fingertips together. "It took me a while to find her. I'd almost given up. You might be interested to know that you led me to her."

"Me?" Bernadette frowned. "Your man was there before me. I never—"

"You did. Leaving her e-mails on your computer at the orphanage—very naive, sweetheart."

Bernadette had almost forgotten the wire in her pocket. Suddenly, she realized her victim had just given her every bit of information she needed. When were the feds going to jump him? Maybe they were waiting for her to get out of the way.

She stood up.

Then Grenville frowned. His gaze was on the zoo entrance. "That young man coming out of the ticket booth looks very familiar. I think you've brought your boyfriend, Bernadette. How very unwise."

Owen kept his distance as the hit man continued to walk along the fence toward a brick-lined bed of shrubs. Surely Osborn's men would take him out soon. But Owen was going to follow anyway, just in case.

A few feet farther down, a row of tall ornamental trees with dense foliage marched along the fence. The assassin melted behind them.

Why had one of the feds not already taken the shot? Now the shooter was behind cover and it would be that much more difficult.

Owen squatted in the deep shade of a tree hanging over the fence as if he were a tourist overcome by the heat. Adjusting his cap, he looked up at the roof of the gift shop, where Osborn had stationed a sniper. What he saw sent his heart banging around in his chest.

A hand dangling over the edge of the flat roof. The FBI sniper had somehow been taken out.

Owen had to get to Grenville's guy before he could fire on Bernadette.

Slowly he rose and prepared to retrace his steps. So far the assassin hadn't seen him. If he could go around to the other side of the fence and approach from behind, maybe he could catch the guy by surprise.

But before he could move, he heard a scream from the picnic area. His head jerked around in time to see Grenville grab Bernadette and jerk her back against him.

He had a split second to make his decision. Osborn's men surrounded Bernadette. But there was nobody to take out the sniper. Nobody but him.

Tearing into a sprint, he launched himself behind the row of ornamental trees. The shooter crouched there, a rifle at his shoulder. Owen dove at him, knocking the gun upward just as he fired. Ears ringing, Owen swung a fist into the man's face and yanked the gun out of his slack hands as he fell.

He stood over the assailant with the rifle braced in both hands. But the guy was out cold. Owen nudged him with his toe to make sure, then threw the gun to the ground and leaned down to flip him over and cuff him.

Shaking, Benny watched Johnny Stapp read Judge Paul Grenville his rights—as if he didn't know them better than anybody else—and escort him toward the zoo's entry plaza. Cops were swarming all over the place by now.

But what had happened to Owen? Just before Grenville

had grabbed her, he'd taken off running toward the row of landscaping along the fence. Then her attention had been focused on fighting against Grenville's hateful touch.

Thank God Stapp and a couple of other agents had quickly subdued her enemy, releasing her to back out of the way and gather her composure. Now that it was over, she felt as if she might collapse into a confused puddle of emotion. Relief warred with frustrated rage that she had been forced to listen to that arrogant jerk preen. But her overwhelming emotion was anxiety for Owen.

She was just about to approach one of the agents standing around with a radio at his mouth when she saw Owen striding toward her with a man slung over his shoulder like a sack of feed. The man's hands were cuffed behind his back, and if she wasn't mistaken, it was the sniper who had killed Ladonna and chased her and Owen all over Mexico.

With a weary grunt, Owen dropped his burden none too gently at the feet of one of the agents. "Book this guy." Dusting his hands off, he walked toward Bernadette.

Relief blasted away her lingering fear. Running toward him, she cast herself at him like a wild woman.

"Owen!" She flung her arms around his neck as he picked her up and swung her in circles. Giddy, she hung on. "Put me down, you're making me dizzy."

"Good. You've been making me pretty cockeyed for a good while and it's about time for a little payback." But he hugged her tightly and slowed until they stood close together. He released her until her feet touched the ground. "Are you okay? I heard him yell, but I was afraid our bozo from Mexico would shoot, so I had to tackle him first."

"I'm fine. Shook up, but he didn't hurt me."

"Did they get what they needed on the wire?"

"I think so. I'm sure of it. He bragged a lot." She shivered and Owen tightened his arms.

"I'm sorry, darlin'. I didn't want you to have to do that."

"I know. But I'm glad I did. He's gone for good now."

He shook his head. "You'll have to testify at the trial. But I'll be there with you."

She leaned back a little. "Will you?"

He smiled the killer dimpled smile she loved so much. "Just try getting rid of me."

"Tell Dean to stick it," said Owen, watching Eli carry Mercedes and Danilo on a tandem horsey ride across the backyard. Sprawled in a lounge chair on the deck with a glass of iced tea at his elbow, he was waiting for Isabel and Bernadette to come back from a shopping trip. Calling the Del Rio station to check in had been a mistake.

"Yeah, right," said Kennedy with a loud snort. "I'd be circling want ads myself by tomorrow morning. He said if you had the nerve to call before Monday, he wanted you back here ASAP."

"He already extended my leave. He can't go back on it. Just pretend you never heard from me."

Kennedy was silent. "Will you trade shifts with me for a week in December? I want to go deer hunting."

"I'll name my firstborn child after you if you'll make sure I get the next few days off. I'm going to ask my girl to marry me this weekend, and I want to do it here in San Antonio."

Kennedy let out a sigh. "I just lost a hundred bucks. Odds were you'd have dumped her by now and moved on to the next babe."

"You'll have to meet her. Then you'll understand."

"Man," said Kennedy, "another one bites the dust."

Owen got off the phone just as Eli plopped into a lawn chair, panting. Both kids were jumping on the trampoline.

"You got reservations all set up with the restaurant?" asked his brother, grabbing his own glass of iced tea. "Boat tickets?"

Owen rolled his eyes. "It's a good thing you've got three other people to organize besides me now. Yes, I have the reservations and the tickets. And the ring." He paused as a curl of anxiety hit his stomach. "Are you sure she won't care that it's not a diamond?"

"If I know Bernadette, she wouldn't care if it was a gumball-machine prize. For some reason, she loves you, my brother." Eli's eyes were soft with affection. "You've earned her. Now quit worrying."

"When do you think they'll be back?"

Eli put his fingers to his temples and closed his eyes. "Umm, I see them leaving the mall right now."

"Oh, shut up." He laughed.

"Relax." Eli winked. "All she can do is say no."

Bernadette watched Owen give the captain/tour guide an exorbitant tip as he helped her off the boat. This time he'd treated her to a dinner cruise catered by one of the famous restaurants along the Riverwalk.

It had been romantic, intimate and sweet. Utterly Owen.

Now that she knew him—saw past the cocky flyboy teasing—she was amazed that she hadn't fallen in love with him a long time ago. Or maybe she *had* loved him all along and just didn't know it.

Whatever the case, tonight he was going out of his way to make her feel like a princess, and she adored him so much that it felt dangerous. For the past two days, which they'd spent resting and recuperating with Isabel and Eli, she'd struggled with the awareness that her life had been completely revolutionized by a collision with Owen Carmichael.

How could she go back to Acuña, settle down at the orphanage and live without him? On the other hand, if he was crazy enough to ask a messed-up woman like her to marry him...

How could she leave her God-given calling to return to the States as a Border Patrol wife?

There seemed to be no easy answer. She was determined to just enjoy this evening with him and figure it out later.

He took her hand as they walked toward the botanical gardens. The air was sweet and heavy with jasmine, mixed with the smell of good food and twined around the slap of water against the banks, music from a mariachi band and laughter from the people around them. She thought of the last time they'd been here, how happy she'd been. But then there'd been a lingering haze of danger and dread.

This time she felt so light and free she could have floated up to the velvet black sky above.

"What are you thinking about?" Owen drew her toward one of the stone bridges arching over the river. They mounted the steps and headed across, swinging hands.

"Just—" unexpectedly her eyes stung and she blinked "—just how happy I am right now. How blessed."

"I'm the one who's blessed." He stopped in the middle of the bridge and kissed her knuckles, his lips lingering warm on her skin.

Her stomach instantly flipped. *How* was she going to let go of him when the time came?

"I never thought I'd say this, but I don't want to go back to Acuña. I miss the children, but this has been such a sweet time."

"Okay, that was more than I asked for," he muttered, looking up.

Confused, she looked around. "Who are you talking to?"

Instead of answering her question, he laced his fingers through hers. "What if you didn't have to go back to Acuña?"

Her heart began to thump hard. "I have to go back. They need me."

"What if—if Nicho and Faye decided to retire and stay as permanent houseparents?"

"That won't happen." She backed away. "Owen, do you know something I don't? Have I been fired?"

"No!" He ruffled his hair, which he'd managed to get back to a color close to his normal streaky blond. "At least I don't think so. I mean—" He groaned. "This isn't going at all like I meant for it to. Eli told me to stick to the script."

"What script?"

"The one where I get down on one knee in the botanical gardens and give you your ring and ask you—" He gulped, his face bright red.

"Owen…we have to talk about this. You can't just up and drop this on me. I'm a planner. I have a calling from God."

"Yeah, well, what about *my* calling? Not the Border Patrol thing. I guess that's negotiable. But He's told me beyond a doubt that I'm called to be your husband. I don't think I'd make a very good missionary."

"You'd make a great missionary, but that's not the—" She had to stop because Owen had put his hands on either side of her face and proceeded to kiss her. By the time he stopped, she'd forgotten her point. "Now where was I?" she said stupidly.

"I don't care. Bernadette, I love you, and I'm pretty sure you love me, too. I would consider it my greatest honor if you'd marry me, and let's figure out the details of who's changing jobs and moving later." He took a breath. "I guess that's as close to the script as I'm gonna get."

She started to laugh. "That's the funniest proposal I've ever heard in my life."

"That's me, the class clown. So will you?" He reached into the back pocket of his jeans and pulled out a little black velvet box. "I almost forgot." He opened the box and took out an elegant topaz ring. "Can I put this on your finger?"

She had trouble seeing his face for the tears in her eyes. "Yes, please. Oh, Owen, I love you so much." Her hand trembled as the cool gold band slid onto her finger. The topaz stone shone warm in the lamplight of the bridge.

He bent down and kissed her again. "I bought you this when we were here before—when I gave you the earrings." He touched the spirals dangling against her neck. "It just looked like something you'd like. But I can give you a diamond, too, if you want one."

She flung her arms around his neck and kissed him hard. "This is the one I want. *You're* the one I want."

"Bernadette." He stroked her back gently with one hand, cupping her head against his shoulder with the other. "You've been through a lot, and I want you to know I'll be patient with the physical side of our relationship. I can wait until you're ready—"

She stopped him with her lips. "I love you," she whispered. "We'll work it out."

EPILOGUE

On the first Saturday in June, the San Antonio River-walk Marriage Island was decorated with sheer drapes of white tulle, white-slatted latticework and pots of peace lily, philodendron and bougainvillea. White-painted wooden folding chairs were lined up in rows with military precision—the groom's brother and sister-in-law having been in charge of organizing the cere-mony—and heavy white candles in hurricane lamps to protect them from the warm river breeze marched down either side of the aisle.

Owen stood at the front of the little platform in his stiff uncomfortable tux, about to spontaneously combust from impatience. When was she going to show up and get this show on the road?

He looked out at the congregation gathered to watch him and Bernadette promise themselves before God to one another. Jack and Meg had come down from Wash-ington, Meg looking cute and motherly with her little bulge poking out in front. Isabel sat in the front row with his mother. Both of them were dabbing at their eyes with tissues. Danilo had already wandered up the aisle, swinging the fake ring pillow by one corner. Good thing Eli, standing next to Owen as best man, had the real one in his pocket.

Suddenly, the music swelled. Mercedes, wearing a lacy white dress and a white hair ribbon, skipped down the aisle with a basket. Beaming like a little ray of sunshine, she tossed handfuls of pink rose petals onto the carpet as she went.

Then he saw her. Bernadette, on the arm of her former pastor from Fort Worth, Ramón Santos, stood at the end of the aisle, looking like a fairy-tale princess. He swallowed aching emotion. She was in white, from misty veil to dainty slippers—God's pure gift to him, Owen.

She came toward him eagerly, joy lighting her dark-flower face. Stocky Ramón almost had to run to keep up. At the end of the aisle, she looked up at Owen, so open and trusting and loving that he wanted to cry.

"Thank You, Lord," he said aloud as he took her hand.

* * * * *

Dear Reader,

Writing Bernadette and Owen's love story has been a soul journey for me. Over the years I have counseled so many Christian women who struggle with issues of shame and condemnation—remnants of an old life before Christ came in. Words never seem to come to me in the right way when I listen to such heartaches, doubts and fears. My natural response is to write a story to illustrate how God deals with our stumbles.

Bernadette is a character who has begged me to complete her story for years. She was outwardly strong and full of faith, but full of inner feelings of inadequacy and unworthiness. The process of creating for her a hero whom God would use to heal those doubts was eminently satisfying. Owen is to me a picture of God's *agape* unconditional love.

The Bible, of course, is full of word pictures of lives transformed by grace. Rahab. Mary Magdalene. The Samaritan woman at the well. It's amazing how we can know "in our heads" that Jesus washes us clean when we come to Him—and then still act in fear. I hope you'll go to the Bible to reread these wonderful stories, and discover anew the hope available in Jesus!

Blessings,

Elizabeth White

DISCUSSION QUESTIONS

1. Why is Benny so careful about appearances? How does this affect her relationship with Owen? Why do you think she "secretly feared him?" What is it about Benny that intimidates Owen?

2. At first Benny is reluctant to tell Owen exactly why she has to go to Memphis. Do you think her self-protective evasion is justified? Why or why not? Think of some times you have concealed truths about your background from friends and/or people you love. What were your reasons for doing so?

3. Talk about different possible motivations—both negative and positive—for sharing one's past failures. Could doing so help a person who is going through difficulties of his or her own? Who are some biblical characters whose former sinful lifestyles are detailed in Scripture? What, if anything, does the Bible say about discretion in giving testimony?

4. At what point in the story do you think Benny begins to work through the painful and humiliating details of her past? How does Owen help her to do so?

5. How realistic do you find Owen's reaction to Benny's revelations about her past? Talk about his process of moving from shock, distaste and anger to compassion. What does the Bible say about our response to a confession of sin?

6. Sometimes Christians who have known the Lord for a long time become hardened to God's miraculous power to change lives. Is it possible to maintain a walk with Christ, even after terrible addictions and moral failures? Spend a few minutes discussing examples of changed lives that you may have witnessed.

7. Do you think Benny is justified in her rage and hatred of Judge Grenville? If you'd been in her shoes, what would you have said to him on the phone when the FBI made her call him? Is it possible to forgive someone who has offended you that grievously? What does the Bible say about confronting those who have wronged us?

8. Benny isn't the only character in the story who has undergone a dramatic transformation. What do you think about the reformation of her former madam, Ladonna Roker? Do you find their relationship realistic? Why or why not?

9. What part does Owen's relationship with his family play in his outlook on life? How does it affect his ability to emotionally connect with Benny?

10. What challenges do you think a couple with the disparate backgrounds Benny and Owen have had will face after they marry? If you were their premarital counselor, what suggestions would you give?

eHARLEQUIN.com

The Ultimate Destination for Women's Fiction

The eHarlequin.com online community is *the* place to share opinions, thoughts and feelings!

- Joining the community is easy, fun and **FREE!**

- Connect with **other romance fans** on our message boards.

- Meet your **favorite authors** without leaving home!

- **Share opinions** on books, movies, celebrities…and *more!*

Here's what our members say:

"I love the friendly and helpful atmosphere filled with support and humor."
—Texanna (eHarlequin.com member)

"Is this the place for me, or what? There is nothing I love more than 'talking' books, especially with fellow readers who are reading the same ones I am."
—Jo Ann (eHarlequin.com member)

Join today by visiting www.eHarlequin.com!

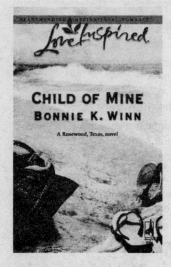